Sherloc
anc
Hammer ... Will

By the same author

Sherlock Holmes
and the
Hammerford Will

John Hall

**BREESE
BOOKS
LONDON**

First published in 2001 by
Breese Books Ltd
164 Kensington Park Road, London W11 2ER, England

© Martin Breese, 2001

ISBN: 0 947 533 98 2

Typeset in 11½/14pt Caslon by
Ann Buchan (Typesetters), Middlesex
Printed in the United States of America

ONE

Mr Sherlock Holmes looked up from his morning post and said, 'Have you any plans for the day, Watson?'

'None at all. Have we a case, then?' I hoped fervently that it was so, for Holmes had been inactive now for a long time, far too long for my tastes. I knew only too well that despite my best efforts over the years the demon still sat leering upon my friend's shoulder. It is true that for a decade now Holmes had not had recourse to anything stronger than rough-cut tobacco or an occasional glass of brandy, but I have seen too many instances in my medical career to believe that dependence upon artificial stimulants can ever be truly eradicated. Let boredom get the better of his resolve for but a moment, and the grinning demon would know that it was the right time to direct Holmes to the syringe in its neat morocco leather case.

By way of an answer, Holmes passed across to me the note which he had been reading, and I looked at it. 'Sir James Damery presents his compliments to Mr Sherlock Holmes, and will call upon him this morning at 10am, if convenient, in connection with a matter of the utmost importance and delicacy. If inconvenient, please advise Sir James at once; he may be contacted at the Carlton Club,' it ran.

'Sounds promising, Holmes.'

'And what do we know of Sir James Damery, then?' mused Holmes, rising from his chair and taking down one of his massive index volumes.

'His name appears constantly in the society pages,' I ventured. 'He is an Irishman, I believe, he certainly has something of a reputation as a dandy, a leader of fashion, and he is often seen in the company of some of the most exalted personages in the land. He began his career as a soldier, or I am much mistaken, and had a fine record.'

'You are not mistaken in the least,' said Holmes, without looking up from the page. 'Here he is, "Colonel Sir James", yes! Irish, as you say, served with an Irish regiment, and with some distinction, rising to command it. H'mm. Left the service some years ago, and does not appear to have done very much since.' He closed the book with a thump, and added in a curious musing tone, 'Or not so far as the press and public are aware, at any rate.'

I asked, 'Oh? And in private?'

Holmes laughed, and threw the volume back on the shelf. 'Ah, that may be a slightly different tale. I have heard some hints, fragments of stories, from Mycroft regarding this Sir James. Reading between the lines, it would appear that he is not merely the companion of some highly placed public figures, just as you said, but their confidant and man of affairs to boot.' He glanced at his watch, raised an eyebrow, and exchanged his shabby old bottle-green dressing gown for a respectable frock-coat. 'Now, Watson,' he went on, 'what does Sir James, Irish aristocrat, distinguished soldier, and latterly doyen of the society pages, a man who has risen so far as to bring himself to the attention of brother Mycroft, want with plain Sherlock Holmes?'

'You should find out soon enough,' I told him, getting up from the table in my turn, 'for that must be his ring at the door now. If the matter is as delicate as both the note and your own knowledge of the man seem to suggest, and especially if it involves important public figures, he will scarcely want me here, so I shall spend the day —'

Holmes raised a hand. 'Sit down, Doctor. He may well be grateful for your opinion, and I know that I certainly shall.'

A moment later, the pageboy ushered Sir James Damery into our little sitting room. My first impression was that the reputation for meticulousness of dress of which I had heard was well-founded. His frock-coat alone must have cost as much as my entire wardrobe, though frankly that is not difficult. His top-hat and shoes did not disgrace the coat, while a large, lustrous pearl glinted in his black silk cravat. But that first glance also made it clear that he was no mere aristocratic waster, not simply a tailor's dummy fit only for escorting beautiful ladies to genteel functions. The grey eyes looked as if they missed nothing, while his deep, rich voice indicated a man used to swaying others by his oratory. This man, I thought, might have been Prime Minister, or an ambassador, had he chosen to turn his energies in that direction. I could not believe that he would ever be content to pass his days drifting idly from club to dinner table.

'I have heard of Doctor Watson, of course,' he said, when Holmes introduced us, 'and shall be grateful if you could stay and listen to my tale, for you may well be of assistance. Particularly,' he added with a smile, 'as you are a fellow-countryman.'

7

'Hardly that, Sir James,' said I.

'Oh, come, now! One Irish grandparent is sufficient to leaven any amount of English dullness. And the same might be said of one French grandparent,' he added, looking at Holmes. 'You see, gentlemen, I have done some research on you. It is as well to know one's friends.'

'And one's enemies?' murmured Holmes.

'That too, of course, if one is unfortunate enough to have 'em.' Sir James laughed, and then grew serious. 'I have said that I have looked into your backgrounds, gentlemen, and that is true. It was a presumption, I know, but a presumption which I am confident you will excuse when you hear the details of the case I am about to lay before you. Suffice it at the outset to say by way of apology that it was essential that I should have complete faith in your discretion.'

'You may rely upon us,' said Holmes.

'Oh, I know that. I should never have contacted you had there been the slightest doubt on that score. Now, to business. Have you heard of the late Lord Hammerford?'

Holmes shook his head. 'Watson?'

'An Irish peer, as I recall? And something of an eccentric, though that is not entirely unknown across the water. That is all that comes to my mind.' I frowned, trying to recollect some gossip I had heard. 'Oh, he died quite recently, did he not? And left a considerable fortune, according to the chap who told me about it. "Rich as Croesus", that was the rather hackneyed phrase he used.'

'That is all perfectly correct, as far as it goes,' said Sir James. He leaned back in his chair. 'The title is an old one, and an honourable one in its own small way. But, as is so often the case with these old families, the lustre outlasted

8

the lucre. To be blunt, the family was all but bankrupt when the late Lord Hammerford succeeded to the title. The estate had shrunk to a fraction of its original size, and what remained was mortgaged and remortgaged to the hilt. The late Lord Hammerford was but a young man when he inherited, still at university. He determined to turn the family fortunes around, threw up his studies and went out to Africa accordingly.

'Well, it was indeed as if the old tale of Croesus, or perhaps King Midas would be a closer parallel, had indeed come true and been brought bang up to date. Gold, diamonds, ivory, sisal, railways, you name it and he made money in it. After a mere decade, he returned home an extremely wealthy man, paid off the creditors, restored the house and grounds to something like palatial splendour, and married the daughter of the local parson. Almost a fairy tale come true, don't you think?'

'Almost,' Holmes agreed.

'The creditors must have been very patient men,' said I.

Sir James laughed aloud. 'It would have cost them more to wind up the estate than they would have recovered!' he told me.

'In that case, Lord Hammerford was fortunate indeed.'

Sir James resumed his tale. 'He settled down, lived quietly, not by any means a recluse, you are to understand, but he went out little in society, preferring to remain with his wife and the one son who was all the family they had. The boy was, as you might expect, the apple of his father's eye, and in this instance the most dispassionate observer could not attribute it to mere parental partiality, for the boy was everything any father might wish, handsome and many-talented. He won his Blue at university, rowed and boxed for his college, was a keen sportsman and swordsman, but never at the expense of his studies, for he took a First. He started with every advantage, and possessed every quality a man might want in his son.

'By the time the son left college, his father had bought not only a town house here in London but an estate in the North of England, which the old Lord Hammerford seldom visited. Anyway, the boy went there to live, and to act as a sort of manager to the estate. The mother was dead by this time, and the two men grew about as close as father and son can be. The lad did what his father had done, married a local clergyman's daughter, and they had one child, a son.' Sir James paused, and looked directly at me. 'You have said that the late Lord Hammerford was a fortunate man, and that was true of the earlier part of his life. And it seemed as if the son, with his manifest and manifold advantages, would be even more blessed. But how inscrutable are the workings of Providence, to quote the Reverend Gilbert White, or someone of that sort. The young wife died in childbirth, and Lord Hammerford's son was heartbroken. A short year later, he too died, a hunting accident.'

'Good Lord!' I said. 'Tragedy almost on a Greek scale.'

Sir James nodded. 'It was dreadful. Now, the only other close family old Lord Hammerford had possessed was a younger brother, who also died suddenly and before his time, and so too did that brother's wife. Their only child was a daughter, old Lord Hammerford's niece, that is to say, and this niece married a man called Sir George Lewis. They had no children of their own, so that one might have expected that the couple would adopt the young boy, look after him. But the — I had almost called it "the curse of the Hammerfords" — that devil's own bad luck which had dogged the family, was at work again. The old Lord Hammerford's niece, now Lady Lewis, had died of cholera on a visit to Venice a short while before, so it was out of the question that the grandson should go there to live.

'The grandfather, the late Lord Hammerford, was by this time very nearly a recluse in reality, burying himself amongst his collection of curios, and passing much of his time studying codes and ciphers, puzzles of all kinds, which had become a hobby of his. It was at that period that he earned that reputation for eccentricity which you mentioned just now, Doctor. He was, as you may imagine, deeply shocked by the death of his one son, another of those untimely deaths which seem so common in the family. Everyone, myself included, fully expected him to withdraw yet further into his shell, and we rather despaired as to what might happen to the grandson. Well, quite unexpectedly, Lord Hammerford, far from withdrawing into it, came out of his shell entirely and took over the upbringing of the grandson, the present Lord Hammerford, himself. He left the Irish estate and moved here to London, saying that the boy needed to be out and about in society, lest he too should run the risk of ending up a recluse. Lord Hammerford still did not mix much in society, preferring to roam the more obscure streets and by-ways, but at least he had emerged from his former isolation, thanks to his grandson. And it worked, against all the odds, and things went on very nicely.' He hesitated.

'Until?' queried Holmes.

Sir James gave a wry smile. 'Until the late Lord Hammerford became ill, a very few weeks ago. I should mention that I was a personal friend, and a week back he called me to his bedside in consequence.' He hesitated a second time.

'Sir James, you have already established that our discretion is to be relied upon,' said Holmes sternly. 'I suggest you stop trifling with words, and set out your case in as succinct a fashion as may be.'

Sir James frowned, then his face cleared. 'You are right, sir,' said he. 'I hesitated just now because it is a very delicate matter, but of course you must know the whole story before you decide what you will do. Well, then, the facts are these. Before ever the grandson was born, the late Lord Hammerford's son and daughter-in-law had all but given up hope of having children.' He looked directly at me. 'As a doctor, sir, you will be only too well aware of the uneasiness, the distress even, which that particular situation can cause.'

'Indeed, yes.'

Sir James nodded. 'Such was the case in this instance. Now, the north country estate was honoured by a visit from a very illustrious personage.' There was a fraction of a second's pause, then he went on, 'I may as well be plain, and say that it was a relative of Her Majesty, and a close relative at that.'

'Ah!' said Holmes, as if it were clear to him.

Sir James nodded. 'I think you have it, Mr Holmes. Need I elaborate?'

'Yes,' said I, 'you need, for I fear you have lost me.'

Sir James sighed. 'Well, Doctor, the person to whom I refer has earned something of a reputation as a ladies' man, if you take my drift, and not entirely undeservedly. To make a plain matter even plainer, do the initials "EP" not suggest anything to you?'

'"EP"? "Ed —" Good Lord!'

Sir James nodded. 'Just so, Doctor. And, a month or so after that visit, the wife told her husband that those wishes which they had almost given up as hopeless dreams had come true at last, and that the family was shortly to be augmented.'

'Good Lord!'

'Indeed,' said Sir James drily. 'Though some might give the credit elsewhere.'

'Ah, I see what you mean, but it may have been mere coincidence,' I told them. 'It need not have meant — well! No, I have known these cases sort themselves out, many a time. Any doctor would tell you exactly the selfsame thing.'

Sir James nodded. 'I would not need telling,' he said. 'Frankly, such a scurrilous thought would never have occurred to me. But the late Lord Hammerford was another matter altogether. He had got the idea into his head that all was not well, if you take my meaning. And nothing that I, or anyone else might say, would shift the notion. Whether it was a result of his illness, his mind becoming unsettled, so to speak, I cannot say. But it is a fact that the idea was planted in his mind and would not be shifted. "Jimmy", says he, he being an old friend of mine, "Jimmy, I've nothing against the man, you'll understand, the family's a good one in its own way, but I should not like my money to go to anyone but a true Hammerford", and I can't say as how I could argue with him there. But for the life of me I couldn't see how the devil he could prove it one way or t'other. And I said as much, plainly, without mincing words, he being an old friend, as I tell you. Well, he levers himself up on the pillow, and he looks at me, and he laughs. "You'll see", he tells me, "when the will's read", and devil another word did he speak in this world.'

'And the will has been read?' Holmes asked.

'It has. You are aware that in English law there is a presumption of legitimacy within marriage. The title goes to the grandson, no question of that, and the real property is entailed, both old and new, so the income from that will provide a competence in any event. The new Lord Hammerford will not be a pauper.' Sir James hesitated again. 'However,' he went on, 'the bulk of the late Lord Hammerford's wealth was his own, earned abroad by his own efforts, just as I told you earlier, and wisely invested since then, and thus he could do what he wanted with it. Well, he chose to convert it into precious stones, and these he hid, somewhere or the other. I have a copy of the will here, and I shall leave it for you to study in detail if you wish to do so, but the gist of it is that the money, or the gems, I should say, which amounts to the same thing, will go to whomsoever is clever enough to find it, or them.'

'Good Lord!' said I, not for the first time during this extraordinary tale. 'Do you tell us that anyone might search for this treasure in gemstones, then? That any casual searcher might recover, and keep, the inheritance rightly due to Lord Hammerford?'

'It is not quite as bad as all that, Doctor,' Sir James told me with a laugh. 'The late Lord Hammerford left two envelopes. One was to be given to the present Lord Hammerford, but the other was to be handed to Sir George Lewis, he being the nearest thing to another relation that old Lord Hammerford had, though he's not a blood relation, for there was no family at all left otherwise. Now, the contents of the envelopes are identical, I have that from the family solicitor, though perhaps he should not have told me. It was old Lord Hammerford's intention that he test his grandson's wits, to see if the new Lord Hammerford is a true descendant or no. I told you that the late lord had a turn for puzzles and cryptograms, did I not? Well, he has left a puzzle to be solved before the treasure is found. If the present Lord Hammerford solves the puzzle and finds the money, well and good, he keeps everything, and incidentally satisfies the late Lord Hammerford's criteria for proof that the inheritance is deserved. But if on the other hand Sir George finds it, the present Lord Hammerford gets merely a pittance, the income from the lands. Now, Mr Holmes, my question to you is just this: will you act for the new Lord Hammerford, assist him to find the treasure, and incidentally avert a possible slander upon both him and a great gentleman to whom we both owe allegiance?'

Holmes sat back in his chair and thought in silence for a long moment. Then he frowned. 'It is an ingenious scheme, I agree,' he told Sir James. 'But there are some points upon which I would wish illumination before making any decision as to whether to help you.'

'Go ahead, Mr Holmes. I am entirely at your disposal.'

'Well, then, I can see that if the parsons are correct in their somewhat gloomy prognostications the late Lord Hammerford might well be satisfied with the outcome of his experiment, one way or the other, as he gazes down from the clouds. But I cannot see that it matters very much to the present Lord Hammerford that his grandfather suspected some irregularity as to that grandson's birth. The money I can understand, for I am not quite so unworldly as to think that wealth is of no importance, but the other matter? You seem to attach some weight to it?'

'Ah, you must understand that if I were the only one to know the background to the will, there would be not the least difficulty, none at all,' said Sir James, a hint of his native brogue creeping into his voice. 'But the late Lord Hammerford told others, not quite so discreet as I. In fact, they are confounded gossips, sir! And they will spread the tale, should Sir George find the treasure first. On the other hand, if the present Lord Hammerford gets the money, well, there may be one or two whispers, but they will soon die down.'

Holmes frowned again, as if he were still not entirely convinced, but said merely, 'I understand. Now, how come you to be involved in all this?'

Sir James looked as close to being embarrassed as was possible for him. 'I have said that the late Lord Hammerford was a good friend. But the other person concerned, a gentleman whom I have the honour to serve as a loyal subject, has also been gracious enough to call me "friend", and I would spare him any unpleasantness, if I possibly can.'

'Well, that is honest enough,' said Holmes. 'But perhaps I phrased my question badly. I meant to ask rather, why is it that the present Lord Hammerford so doubts his wit, native, inherited, or otherwise, that he shies away from an honest attempt to solve the puzzle himself? And, having done so in the first instance and sought an expert opinion on the matter, why does he permit you to act for him? Why, in a word, has he not seen fit to consult me himself?'

Sir James's face flushed, but he kept his voice level as he answered. 'As to acting himself,' he told Holmes, 'he cannot, and there's an end to it. As to his not coming here in person, he has. In fact, he is downstairs, and I'll have him brought up to see you.'

Holmes looked puzzled. 'Oh?'

Sir James went on, 'I have perhaps inadvertently misled you as to the chronology of all this, Mr Holmes. It is true that I have referred to "old" Lord Hammerford, but that was by way of what the doctor here, and his literary colleagues, would perhaps label "elegant variation", and I meant "the late" Lord Hammerford rather than "the aged" Lord Hammerford. The man was no older than I am myself. It is equally true that the late Lord Hammerford drew up this very curious will as soon as he knew of the expected arrival of his grandson. But he evidently believed, and quite reasonably so, that the grandson would have reached his majority by the time the old Lord Hammerford himself died. He was wrong, in the event, for the illness which killed him came upon him quite suddenly and unexpectedly. The will was actually made comparatively recently, less than five years ago now. The present Lord Hammerford is only four years old!'

Before Holmes or I could properly take this statement in, Sir James had risen from his seat and pulled at the bell rope. When Billy appeared, Sir James gave a few instructions, and a moment later a pretty young nursemaid arrived to brighten our little sitting room. She brought with her a little golden-haired lad, who stared at the strangers with wide eyes.

'This,' Sir James told us, 'is Lord Hammerford.' He bent

down and faced the lad squarely. 'Now, young man, this is your Uncle Sherlock, and that is your Uncle John. What they want to know is just this: do you wish them to act for you in the matter of your grandfather's treasure?'

The boy thought a moment, said, 'Yes, Uncle Jimmy,' then put his thumb in his mouth.

Sir James stood up, and nodded to the young nursemaid. 'Take him to the kitchen,' he told her, 'and give him some cocoa, or whatever it is that he drinks. When you're finished there, you can take him home in the carriage. I don't think I'll have finished my business with these gentlemen by the time you leave, but you might look in to say that you're going, and if I'm not done then, I'll walk home when I have, so you need not bother to wait. Well, gentlemen,' he went on as the door closed, 'what do you say? Will you act for young Lord Hammerford, and for me, and for the gentleman whose name we'll not mention?'

I have seen Mr Sherlock Holmes in some tight corners. I have seen him quite literally fight for his life, and maintain a dignified composure throughout. I have even seen him, though only once or twice, at a temporary loss for words. But never have I seen him flounder quite so helplessly as he did then. He waved a limp hand at Sir James, sank into an armchair, and groped weakly for the nearest briar pipe.

'It's evidently something of a shock,' I told Sir James.

'Indeed. Well, Mr Holmes?'

Holmes packed tobacco into his pipe, and looked at me. 'Watson?'

'Holmes has covered much of the ground,' I told Sir James, 'and I'm sure he will have many more questions should we decide to take your case. But he has omitted to get an answer on one of the most significant points, so I will just ask you this. We have spoken lightly of a "treasure", as if we all knew its value, but in point of fact you have not told us just what it may be worth. Would it be in order to ask how much we are actually talking about?'

Sir James drew a memorandum book from his pocket. 'I have only the figures at which the various stones were originally purchased, of course,' he told me, 'but I think it will serve for our purposes. The actual total is a whisker short of half a million pounds.'

TWO

'Half a million pounds!' I fairly gasped it out, and felt obliged to sit down when I had said it, realizing how Holmes must have felt a moment earlier.

'Just a trifle less,' Sir James Damery repeated. 'As I have said, the late Lord Hammerford was a very wealthy man.'

'You did say so,' said Holmes, 'but you failed to mention that he was quite that wealthy.'

'Why,' I added, 'if the present Lord Hammerford finds the treasure, he will be one of the richest men in England. Richest boys, rather.'

'In the world, Doctor,' Sir James corrected me calmly. 'In the world. And of course,' he added, 'the same applies to Sir George Lewis.'

'It occurs to me that this "treasure" of yours must occupy a quite considerable space,' said Holmes thoughtfully.

Sir James laughed. 'You evidently have no notion as to what the jewellers charge these days, Mr Holmes! Were you married, you would know differently, I assure you. And then the late Lord Hammerford was selective, he bought antique carved gems, first quality diamonds, the very best, and most expensive, of everything. A decent-sized hatbox, I fancy, would hold the whole lot. Two hatboxes, perhaps.' He looked from Holmes to me. 'Well, gentlemen? How say you, will you take the case?'

I would not have believed that Holmes could, or would, hesitate for a moment, but he did. 'I am not sure,' he told Sir James.

'You disappoint me, Mr Holmes.'

'And me,' I added, with some astonishment.

Holmes laughed. 'We have all been, and are being, very frank,' he said, 'and so I will not prevaricate now. Had you come to me, Sir James, with the proposition that I should help this lad solve a puzzle, a cipher, to find his inheritance, I should not have hesitated for a moment. But this other business, trying to find a fortune to establish one's legitimacy? And in the process to clear a great man of some suspected illicit liaison? It is outside my usual purview, to speak plainly. The whole scheme has about it a hint of dubiousness, of chicanery. And moreover, having once accepted the challenge, the employment of an agent has more than a hint of cheating, if not downright fraud.'

'And yet you have acted in some delicate personal matters before now,' Sir James reminded him. 'The Kings of Bohemia and Scandinavia might testify as to that.'

Holmes remained unconvinced. 'Quite different, Sir James, I assure you. Why, suppose for one moment that the late Lord Hammerford's wretched suspicions were justified? Should I in my turn be justified in perpetuating a lie by finding this treasure for the boy and having all the gossips believe that which is untrue?'

By this time I could scarcely contain myself. Before Sir James could speak, I answered for him. 'As to that, Holmes, what on earth does it matter? Some of the most respected coats of arms in the land bear the bend sinister, and some of the noblest houses could not in all conscience swear that there were no branches missing from the family tree. Or that there were no cuckoos nesting amongst those branches which remain.'

'True enough,' said Sir James. 'My own family has its share of rascals and rapparees. More than its share, if truth be told. And it is always the biggest rogues whose names are longest remembered.'

'Indeed,' I went on, warming to my task, 'a pride in the little quirks of one's ancestry is the mark of the true Englishman. Do you yourself not boast of an ancestor who was related to Vernet, the French painter?'

'Not boast. Hardly "boast", Doctor,' murmured Holmes. 'But a quiet pride, perhaps that is the right phrase, yes. And when you bring the matter up,' he added, looking at me with a twinkle in his eye, 'I have frequently heard tales of a navy surgeon called Watson, who fought at Trafalgar, and named his son "Horatio", a name which passed down to both grandsons. Yes, I am all but convinced. But I ask you again, Sir James,' he added in a more serious tone, 'does your conscience not trouble you that you have called me in? As I understand you, the will specifies that the two heirs presumptive, if it be accurate so to call them, are to use their wits to find the gems. How does that sit with consulting a third party, an independent expert?'

'Why, the lad's only four! He can hardly be expected to run about London looking for the gems himself,' said Sir James. 'Sir George Lewis will not scruple to use fair means or foul in his search, I assure you. What say you, friend Watson?'

'Delightful little chap,' said I. '"Uncle John", indeed.

Well, I wouldn't mind being —' I broke off as I caught Holmes's cold and cynical eye. 'No need to stare at me like a dead cod, Holmes. This pretence of indifference to the finer emotions is all very well, but it was only last week that I saw the children of your relative, young Doctor Verner, riding on your back. As I recall it they told me that you were a helephant, and the hearth rug was the Sarah Desert.'

Holmes looked as if he were about to make some scathing reply to this, when he could think of one, but he was saved the trouble by the young nursemaid, who tapped on the door and looked in to say that she was about to leave with young Lord Hammerford.

'Ah, I've not quite finished here,' said Sir James. 'You take the carriage, and I'll walk back later.' As the nursemaid nodded and turned, he added, 'Wait a moment, though. I'll see you to the carriage, for I think Mr Holmes would appreciate being left alone with his thoughts for a while.'

'I'll go too,' said I. 'Let Holmes stew in his own juice for a time.' This was, I assure you, my only motive. I was, to speak plainly, disappointed that Holmes's reaction had been lukewarm at best, and genuinely thought that a moment's private reflection might induce him to change his mind. Should any sour old cynic think that I had some sentimental wish to see a bit more of the young lad — or, for the matter of that, the young nursemaid — then that is a matter for the cynic concerned.

Sir James and I accompanied the girl to the bottom of the stairs, where Mrs Hudson, looking positively motherly, was trying to induce young Lord Hammerford to repeat some nursery rhyme after her. She looked up as we reached them, coughed to hide her embarrassment, and mumbled something about having things to do in the kitchen.

I said a last farewell to the young aristocrat, and he gravely held up his hand for me to shake it. The nursemaid took Lord Hammerford out to the carriage, and Sir James went with them, while I stood in the doorway.

Sir James was just about to hand Lord Hammerford in when a large, rough-looking man who had been lounging nearby suddenly pushed Sir James aside, and made as if to snatch the boy. As I have indicated, Sir James was not the languid and effete aristocrat of popular imagination, but an old soldier, a man of action. He was thrown off balance for a second, then recovered himself and raised his stick in a threatening fashion.

Meanwhile, having recovered from my own surprise, I had rushed from the doorway to give what assistance I might. At the same time the coachman, who had the appearance of a former prize-fighter, was climbing down from his seat with a purposeful look on his face, and a salty phrase or two of reproof on his tongue. The rough-looking man, seeing Sir James's stick descending towards him, and reinforcements on the way, so to speak, quickly concluded that discretion was the proverbially better part of valour and took to his heels.

The nursemaid hugged young Lord Hammerford, who had burst into tears. I looked at Sir James, and Sir James looked at me. 'Shall I go after him?' I asked.

The coachman, who had started off after the rough and chased him for a few paces, returned and shook his head. 'Sorry, sir, can't catch him,' said he. 'He's at the end of the road now.'

It was true. For a big man, the would-be kidnapper had

moved remarkably fast. I glanced around for a policeman. I could not see one, but a man in a commissionaire's uniform had seen the commotion and was making his way towards us, and I recognized him. 'Look here, Peterson,' I told him, 'some villain has just attempted to make off with this young chap. Would you be a good fellow and ride along with them, just to be on the safe side?'

Peterson readily agreed, and with him and the coachman on the alert I had few fears for the safety of the little party. Sir James and I watched the carriage until it turned the corner, then looked at one another. 'Holmes should be told of this,' said I. 'It may have some bearing on this other business.'

'I think you are right, Doctor. And I think I might venture to hazard a guess as to just what that bearing is.' Sir James led the way up to our sitting room, where Holmes was sunk in an armchair, his pipe emitting great clouds of smoke.

He glanced up as we entered the room, all badly suppressed excitement. 'I — hello! What's the matter, then?'

'Holmes, an attempt has just been made to kidnap young Lord Hammerford,' I told him.

'What?' He fairly roared it out.

'Yes,' said Sir James, 'and I think I know who was behind it.'

Holmes waved a hand for silence, then asked me for an account of what had happened, which I gave him in a few words. He was silent for a moment, then looked at me gravely. 'You are satisfied that the boy is safe?'

'I am, Holmes. Peterson is with them, and the coachman looks as if he'd be pretty handy in a scrap. But I think you will agree that this alters things slightly.'

He nodded. 'It does indeed, Watson.'

I went on, 'Of course we must take his case. As you yourself said, if it had been a mere abstract problem, there would not have been a moment's hesitation on your part. Then this kidnap attempt shows that he is in serious danger, and there can be no doubt in anyone's mind that the inheritance is somehow at the back of it. And as a final point, if you're still concerned about this nonsense of his relying on his own wits, I should have thought that by asking you to take the matter in hand on his behalf the lad showed first-class judgement. Nothing wrong with his mind there, Holmes. If that isn't using his wits, then what is, pray? By my way of thinking, that circumstance alone is proof enough, not that proof were needed, that the lad is a true Hammerford.'

Holmes shrugged his shoulders in mock resignation. *'Vox Watsoni, vox Dei est,'* he told Sir James. 'We accept the case, thanks to the would-be kidnapper, and not to you, Sir James. And I note, where Watson evidently does not, the fact that you had clearly put the lad up to replying as he did.'

'Why, of course I did! What the devil does such a young boy know of the wicked world, or yet of you, Mr Holmes? But what of the kidnapper?'

'The rough ran off at a fair speed, Holmes,' I added. 'We did not think it worth pursuing him.'

'But I can tell you who put him up to it!' cried Sir James.

'Indeed?'

'Indeed. It must have been Sir George.'

'Sir George Lewis, the relative by marriage and rival claimant under the terms of the will?'

'None other. Who else would have any reason to harm the lad?'

Holmes shook his head. 'These are deep waters, Sir James. Deeper than you had led me to believe.' He sat up. 'But that is all to the good, from your point of view, for it gives me a reason to take an interest in the matter.'

'I am gratified to hear it, Mr Holmes. Good has come out of evil, which is a rare thing in this wicked world. But I was sure you would take the case, sir.' Sir James rubbed his hands with delight. 'And Mycroft agreed with me.'

'Oh? You have spoken to my brother, then?'

'He is an old friend,' Sir James told him, 'and I consulted him before ever I thought of you. He solved the riddle, by the way, but was disinclined to take the matter further, muttering something about "trouble in the Balkans", for all the world as if there were ever anything else there. "If Sherlock cannot help", he told me, "you may call upon me again a week on Tuesday, when things are quieter, and I shall explain it all to you", and he waved me away. He did not even tell me what the riddle meant, but I could tell by his face that he had solved it. Or the first one, I should say, for I suspect there will be a considerable trail to follow before we find the treasure.'

'Ah, the riddle, yes,' said Holmes, evidently nettled that Sir James had only considered him as a second choice. 'We had best take a look at that.'

Sir James took a sheet of paper from his memorandum book, and passed it to Holmes, who read it thoughtfully before asking, 'And you say that Sir George Lewis has an identical clue to this?'

Sir James nodded. 'So says the family solicitor, an old friend of mine.'

Holmes passed the paper to me. 'Watson?'

I read aloud, '"Where to begin? Why, from whence!" Extraordinary, Holmes!'

'Elementary, rather. Though not entirely devoid of interest. You say that Lord Hammerford has, or had, rather, a house here in London?' he asked Sir James.

'Yes, in Mayfair. It was there that he spent his last days.'

'I thought as much. The clue is the word, "whence", of course. If we consider only the pronunciation and not the spelling, we may easily derive the word "wen", long a favourite among would-be humorists and punsters to mean London. Not a riddle that would tax even Mycroft's ingenuity, so I do not doubt that he solved it at a glance.' This thought seemed to mollify Holmes somewhat. He added caustically, 'I thought you said the late Lord Hammerford was something of an expert in riddles? I see little evidence of that here, to be plain.'

'I said that he was keen on them,' said Sir James defensively. 'I did not say that he was any good at making them up.'

'I should have thought that the fact that the riddles are simple to solve would make our task that much easier,' I put in.

Holmes shook his head. 'On the contrary, it makes our task that much harder, for it means that the man who moves fastest, and not the cleverest man, has the advantage.' He waved the piece of paper at Sir James. 'When did you acquire this, pray?'

'Last night. I visited Mycroft, but when I left him it was too late to decently call upon you.'

'And this Sir George Lewis had his clue at the same time? So he has almost a day's start upon us? You have been very remiss, Sir James, in not consulting me sooner.'

'I still don't see that it gets us very far, Holmes,' said I. 'London is a pretty big place, after all.'

He sighed. 'We can, I think, narrow it down slightly, Watson. I fancy we shall find the next clue — such as it is — at Lord Hammerford's town house.' And he made as if to get up.

'Hardly that, Holmes!' I told him.

He resumed his seat, and gazed cynically at me. 'You have an alternative solution to the riddle, Watson?'

'Oh, no. I would never have thought of the answer. But, now that you have explained it means we are to look right here in London, I see clearly that it cannot be the house which is meant.'

'Indeed?'

'Indeed. Sir James, did you not say the entire real property was entailed, and thus passes at once to the young Lord Hammerford?'

'I did, Doctor.'

'There you are, then. If the house is Lord Hammerford's, then this Sir George could not guarantee that he would be admitted. If the test is to be a fair one, the two of them must have an equal chance of access to the next clue.'

To give him credit, Holmes leaned back in his chair and clapped his hands. 'First blood to you, Watson. Well done! You are right, of course, it must be a public place. And yet,' he went on, half to himself, 'it must not be too public, or else anyone might stumble on the treasure, or the next clue, purely by chance. Somewhere that shares both public and private qualities, then. But where?'

'A library, perhaps?' I cried. 'Oh, no. Too public, any

casual browser might find the clue if it were tucked away inside a book. I know, Holmes — a club!'

He nodded. 'Well done again. You are right, of course. Was the late Lord Hammerford a member of any London clubs?' he asked Sir James.

'He was. And there can be no ambiguity, for he was only a member of the one club. I can take you there, if you wish, for I'm a member myself.'

In a very few minutes we were rattling along in a cab. As we moved off, both Holmes and I began to speak to Sir James. We laughed, apologized to one another, and I waved to Holmes to continue.

'Thank you, Watson. Now, Sir James, you said, I think, that this Sir George Lewis would use "fair means or foul" to succeed. Did you mean that quite literally, I wonder? Is he likely to be a danger to us?'

'Well, my first thought was that it was he who induced that fellow to try to snatch young Lord Hammerford. You seemed to think not, though?'

Holmes shook his head. 'I have my reasons for thinking otherwise. But what of Sir George Lewis? Is he a rogue?'

Sir James reflected for a moment before replying. 'I'll not say he's a rogue, for I know nothing definite against the man. In fact, now I think about it, this dirty kidnapping business is not his way at all. I have no doubt that you're right there, Mr Holmes, though I'm damned if I know how you knew. But for all that there are some questions which one might wish answered about Sir George.'

'Such as?'

'The first is the matter of his wife's death, his first wife, that is, the niece of the late Lord Hammerford.'

'I thought she died of the cholera, in Venice?' Holmes said.

'That is so. He had her buried there, though.'

'Understandable, with the cholera,' I told him. 'He would not want her brought home by sea, even if the authorities permitted it.'

'Oh, I grant you that,' said Sir James. 'Still it's out of the ordinary, for none of the family attended the funeral, apart from Sir George himself, that is.'

'But you said there was no family?' Holmes put in.

'The late Lord Hammerford was alive at the time, and would have gone, I am certain. Although, in fairness to the man, time was against him with its being the cholera, just as Doctor Watson says. Communications from the Continent are by no means as speedy as one might wish at the best of times. We'll give him that, then. But then he remarried with almost indecent haste on his return to England.'

'When you say "indecent haste", what time-scale do you imply?' asked Holmes.

'Oh, a year. Two.'

'Hardly indecent haste, Sir James,' I could not help saying. 'I have known many loving husbands who were utterly devastated by the death of their wives, but yet felt such loneliness, such despair, that they remarried almost at once, on the rebound, so to speak.'

'Well, I said I knew nothing specific against him, and I'll repeat that. But it's a curious little incident, to my way of looking at it. The man's chronically short of cash, that much is a fact. He plays the horses, and the markets, but with little success. Half a million, nay, a couple of thousand, would help him out quite considerably.'

'That's hardly conclusive proof of villainy,' I said. 'Why, I'd settle for a couple of hundred myself at the moment.' The other two looked curiously at me. 'Sir George isn't the only one to have a losing streak on the Turf,' I explained.

'Ah!' said Sir James. 'Nevertheless, Sir George needs cash badly just at the moment. That means that he may not play fair.'

'H'mm. It is a powerful motive to bend the rules, I agree,' said Holmes. He looked at me. 'I interrupted you earlier, Watson?'

'Oh, my question was just about young Lord Hammerford. What's to become of him now, with no family to look after him?'

Sir James's brow clouded. 'I've been troubled over that myself, Doctor. But, if it comes to the push, my wife and I will look after him. He's staying with us for the time being, of course. We're getting a bit long in the tooth, and have no children of our own, but still I'll not see him given to some stranger to look after. Delightful little chap, you'll agree?'

'Oh, absolutely! If my own wife were still alive, then of course —' and I stared out of the carriage window, while the others kept a discreet silence for the rest of the journey.

We turned into a quiet street in St James's, and stopped before a mighty oak door which bore no nameplate. Holmes got out of the carriage, and rubbed his hands together eagerly, the thrill of the chase writ large upon his features. 'One last question,' he asked Sir James, as we stood upon the pavement, 'is Sir George Lewis a small man, with a weaselly look about him?'

'Good God, no! Whatever makes you think that? No, Sir George is a gentleman, and looks the part, whatever else you may say of him. He's a good six foot, an athlete — he's an amateur rider and boxer, you know. Handsome, or so the ladies tell me, though I'm not a judge of that myself, of course.' He frowned. 'Why do you ask?'

'Because we have been followed by a man of the description I gave you,' said Holmes calmly.

'Are you sure?'

'Positive. He was lurking in Baker Street when we left the rooms, and he has followed us here in a cab — no! Don't look round, man. Now, if it is not Sir George, then there are two possibilities left.'

'Which are?' asked Sir James.

'Well, we shall leave that for the moment.' Holmes took a step towards the great oak door.

'Holmes,' said I, 'I hesitate to throw cold water on these proceedings, but a gentlemen's club is a pretty big place. Are we to search all the rooms, or what?'

'I hardly think that will be necessary,' said Holmes. 'Unless Sir George himself is a member, he would not be able to enter to carry out such a search, and you yourself pointed out that fairness was of the essence. Is there a doorman, or commissionaire, or anyone of that sort, Sir James?'

'A doorman,' said Sir James, ushering us inside, and indicating a little counter affair in the lobby. 'Gentlemen, this is Mortimer, who keeps the club members in good order.'

We nodded at the doorman, an ancient fellow who looked as if he had been sitting behind his counter since the club was founded a century ago. He was dressed in a rusty-coloured uniform, but his eye was alert, even merry, and he regarded us with some amusement. 'Sir James, nice to see you again, sir,' said he, struggling to lever himself out of the wicker chair in which he sat.

'Don't trouble yourself to get up, Mortimer,' said Sir James. 'Mortimer, this is Mr Sherlock Holmes, and Doctor Watson.'

'Indeed, Sir James?' The old fellow clambered to his feet at that, and held out a hand. 'I've read of your adventures, of course, gentlemen. Pleased to meet you both, I'm sure. Might I venture to ask if you are putting them up for membership, then, Sir James? I know the secretary would regard it as an honour for the club.'

'Not at the moment. Unless, that is, you'd want it, gentlemen? No? No, Mortimer, we're here on a rather odd errand, in connection with the unfortunate death of the late Lord Hammerford, whom you knew.'

'Indeed I did, sir. And may I make so bold as to express the deep regret which I, and the rest of the staff, felt at the sad news? Anything I can do, of course, Sir James, you have but to name it, sir.'

Sir James nodded, but looked at something of a loss. 'Mr Holmes, perhaps you had best outline our problem?'

Holmes leaned over the little counter, and addressed the doorman in a low tone. 'Mr Mortimer, did the late Lord Hammerford leave anything with you, to be called for?'

The old fellow rubbed his hands with glee. 'Yes, indeed, Mr Holmes.' He reached under the counter, and took out a large white envelope, marked 'HAMMERFORD', and nothing more, on the outside. 'I must say, gents, that's a load off my mind, with both having been called for now.'

'Both?' asked Holmes sharply. 'The second — or perhaps I

should say, the first — envelope has been called for, then?'

'Damnation!' said Sir James.

Mortimer regarded the aristocratic figure like the stern father of fiction studying a headstrong but much-loved son, then addressed himself to Holmes. 'This very morning, sir.' He glanced at the old grandfather clock which stood in a corner. 'Not above an hour since, either.'

'And by whom, pray?'

'Gent didn't give no name, sir. A tall gentleman, well set up, the sort as would turn the head of any lady's maid, or the lady herself, for the matter of that.'

Sir James made as if to speak, then subsided, but I knew well enough what was in his mind, for a similar thought had occurred to me.

Holmes went on, 'I see. And what did this gentleman do? Just ask for the envelope and go?'

'More or less, sir. He ripped it open, stood more or less where you might be standing now, he was, and read the letter that was in it. Then his face changed, so to speak, an odd look come over him.'

'How, "odd"?' asked Holmes.

'If you was to ask me to put a name to it, sir, that name would be "bafflement",' said Mortimer. 'Baffled, he looked. Then he swore, using much the same unfortunate terms as Sir James used just now, shoved the envelope and letter in his pocket, and walked out.'

'Walked, rather than ran?'

'Strolled, Mr Holmes, for all the world like a man with a lot on his mind, if you'll forgive the familiar phrase.'

'Ah, that must be a good sign,' said Holmes. 'Well, then, let us see if we are as baffled as Sir — as the other gentleman.'

But he did not rush to open the envelope, instead studying it closely first. When he had done this to his satisfaction, he took out his penknife, slit the envelope carefully, and took out the sheet of paper it contained, a single, ordinary sheet of notepaper, folded twice. Holmes unfolded this slowly, and looked at it for a moment, without speaking.

Now, Holmes possesses self-restraint to a far greater extent than any other man I know, and a casual observer would have seen no change in his face. But I, who knew him of old, could tell that he too was puzzled, 'baffled', even. After a long moment, he laughed aloud.

'Well?' I demanded.

'Well, I expected some mystery, perhaps even some difficulty, and I am not so egotistical as to exclude entirely the possibility that even our combined best efforts might meet with failure at the last. But I confess that I had not expected the trail to go cold quite so quickly,' said Holmes. And he held out before the astonished Sir James and me — a blank sheet of paper!

THREE

'**D**amnation!' said Sir James a second time.

'The clues appear to be getting harder,' said I.

Holmes shot me a venomous glance.

'Sympathetic ink, perhaps?' I suggested, trying to make some amends for my levity.

Holmes frowned. He held the sheet up and sniffed at it, then went over to the door, held it up to the light and looked at it closely. 'A logical enough surmise, Watson, but I think not,' said he after all this. 'Most of the common preparations have a faint but distinctive odour, and there is none here that I can detect. Moreover, however close to "invisible" an ink may be, it must needs be applied with a pen nib, and the trained observer may detect the damage to the surface fibres of the paper quite easily. This sheet shows no trace of any impression, not even the faint marks which would show that it had been placed underneath another sheet upon which a message had been written in pencil, another possibility which had, I am certain, suggested itself to you. No, it must be the actual paper which is the clue, although it seems quite ordinary to the casual observer.'

'Or the envelope?' I suggested.

'H'mm. Again, an ordinary enough envelope. Sir James,

the name "Hammerford" is written in rather straggling capitals, as you see. Is that the late Lord Hammerford's writing?'

Sir James studied the envelope closely. 'I cannot say that it is not,' he said at length. 'It is true that it is very different from his usual hand, which was a neat, if somewhat old-fashioned, copperplate. I have never known him use capitals like that, but I cannot swear that it is not his doing.'

'H'mm,' said Holmes again. To me, who knew him well, the signs were obvious; he was irked by his lack of progress. 'Mortimer, can you swear that this was the very same envelope which Lord Hammerford left with you?'

'That I can, Mr Holmes.'

'There can be no possibility that someone has taken the original and left a substitute?'

'None at all, sir. I have my eye on them constantly. Had, I should say.'

'You cannot be here at your desk twenty-four hours a day, though?'

'No, sir, but when I goes off duty, I takes, or took, I ought to say, those two envelopes with me, that being Lord Hammerford's wish. "If they can't come here during the day like gentlemen, Mortimer", says he, "then they don't deserve any success anyway", no offence gentlemen, but those was his own words, and he goes on to tell me to keep them letters under my eye at all times. Which, as I say, I did.'

'I see.'

'Holmes,' I ventured, 'is there any significance in the fact that capital letters are used, think you? Capitals, the capital, London — damn! We'd worked that one out already. Still,' I added doubtfully, 'it might serve as confirmation. Though it takes us no further.'

'No, I hardly think the superscription is intended as an elaborate red herring, Watson.'

'Well, then, how about "block", as in "block capitals"?' I persisted. 'In the American usage, that would surely direct us to the corner of the street?'

'I don't think that is the answer either,' said Sir James with a laugh. 'The late Lord Hammerford was not quite so familiar with American usage as you, Doctor.'

'And, begging your pardon, Doctor,' added Mortimer, 'there isn't anything on the corner, in either direction. Just blank walls.'

'Blank walls? And a blank sheet of paper. Nothing in that at all, Holmes?'

I got a very impatient shake of the head by way of reply.

'Very well,' I persisted, 'the sheet of paper was folded twice, when it need only have been folded once, if at all, to go into the envelope. Perhaps the second street corner?'

A shadow of a smile appeared on Mortimer's face as he watched us flounder. He shook his aged head. 'Nothing to the right, sir, except the square. To the left, let me see, well, there's a little tobacconist's shop.'

'Ah, that might be more like it,' said I.

It was Sir James's turn to shake his head. 'I don't believe that the late Lord Hammerford had ever been inside a tobacconist's shop in his life,' he told me, 'for he detested the habit. Being a gentleman, of course, he never imposed his own very limited views on others, never tried to dissuade his friends from smoking,' and he offered me his cigar case as he said the words, 'but certainly he never smoked himself.'

'That in itself might be a clue, then,' I said, reluctant as ever to abandon my own theory. 'The odd, the unusual, that is what we must look for.'

Holmes gave an impatient click of the tongue. 'This is really very vague and insubstantial stuff, Watson,' said he. 'No, I am sure that the clue is in this sheet of paper itself. A blank sheet. Blank. Nothing on it. Nothing, there's the clue. Nothing, nobody, nowhere — nowhere, of course! Mortimer, was there another set of two envelopes, or something of the sort?'

The old fellow came as close to laughing aloud as his gravity would permit. 'You have it, sir!' he told Holmes. 'I'll have to rummage in my little cubbyhole, though, for I keep the others safe in there. If you'll excuse me —' and he broke off abruptly as the door was roughly opened and a tall man burst into the little lobby.

'I say, Mortimer, or whatever your name is — oh!' The newcomer broke off abruptly as he saw us standing there. He was about six feet in height, nearer forty than thirty years of age, with a handsome though slightly dissipated face. He stopped before the little counter, and nodded a greeting. 'Sir James, delightful to meet you again.'

Sir James stiffened, then seemed to recollect his manners, and said, 'Sir George Lewis, may I present Mr Sherlock Holmes and Doctor John Watson?'

We exchanged the usual pleasantries, after which Sir George seemed at a loss for a moment. He quickly recovered himself, though, and told us, 'I see that Sir James, good soldier that he is, has brought up his reserves. Or should I perhaps say his heavy guns? You have evidently solved the first puzzle, gentlemen.'

'And the second,' said Holmes calmly. 'Just as you have.'

'Ah. Indeed.' Sir George did not turn a hair. 'Mortimer, it had occurred to me that perhaps you had a second envelope, or something of that sort. It appears I was correct?'

'One moment, Sir George, if you please. I was just about to get one for Mr Holmes, but this'll save my poor old legs,' and he tottered off into the dark recesses of what he had termed his 'cubbyhole', a sort of pantry affair in a corner behind the desk. We stood in embarrassed silence for a moment or two. At any rate, I felt embarrassed at having Sir George stand there beside me, and I sensed that Sir James was none too happy. Anyway, the others said nothing as we stood there for what seemed an age, until Mortimer eventually returned with a couple of white envelopes, apparently identical to the one we had just opened except that these bore no superscription. He made an awkward little attempt at a formal bow, and handed one of the envelopes to Holmes, and the other to Sir George. 'There you are, gents, both alike, just as old Lord Hammerford wished it.'

'Thank you,' said Sir George. He tapped the envelope against his chin, hesitated, then said, 'I don't suppose you have a third set of envelopes, Mortimer? Just to save me another journey?'

Mortimer laughed, and set himself coughing. 'More envelopes yet? Bless you, sir, no. Just the two sets of envelopes. Two lots of envelopes, them's all the envelopes I ever had to look after. And glad to get rid of, for I was forever worrying about 'em going missing. Been a weight on my mind, they have, a real worry. A heavy responsibility, as you might venture to say,' he added significantly, with a delicate little cough.

'Ah, right you are.' Sir George rummaged in his pocket, and produced a handful of silver. 'Bit short, just at the moment, but very grateful and all that,' and he crossed Mortimer's wrinkled and outstretched palm.

Holmes too passed a small token of his appreciation to the old doorman, then gazed from his envelope to that which Sir George held. 'Should we perhaps say, "One, two, three, go!" and tear them open together?' he asked.

Sir George laughed. 'I'm game if you are.'

'On a somewhat more serious note, Sir George, I think we would be as well to have a little talk before we proceed further,' said Holmes. 'Perhaps we might find somewhere a little more private?'

'We can use the sitting room here,' said Sir James. 'I'm a member, as I told you, and there's not usually anybody much in there through the day.'

'Sir George?'

'That suits me, Mr Holmes.' Sir George's tone showed that he was intrigued, but he said nothing more as Sir James led us into the darkness of the club, down a short passage and up a shallow stair into a gloomy and dusty sitting room. There was but one occupant, a very old gentleman looking like a retired army man, who snored loudly in a leather armchair in one corner.

'The General won't disturb us before luncheon,' said Sir James, waving us to seats. 'Shall I ring for the steward?'

'Nothing for me at present,' said Holmes.

'Nor me, thank you,' said Sir George. 'And now, Mr Holmes, what had you in mind?'

'Well, to speak bluntly, I had in mind a pooling of resources,' said Holmes.

'Mr Holmes!' Sir James Damery had evidently not expected to hear this, and equally evidently it was not greatly to his taste when he did hear it.

Sir George laughed. 'I think that's your answer, Mr Holmes! Even if I were to agree, Sir James here never would.'

'It might be unwise to decide too hastily,' said Holmes. 'You, Sir George, solved the first clue an hour or so before we did, but then you lost your advantage when we realized that a blank sheet of paper meant that the third clue was to be found in the same place as the second. I can easily picture the quite ridiculous situation in which we play leap-frog, metaphorically speaking, with each party arriving just as the other has found the next clue. It is undignified, and it gives too much weight to the vagaries of blind chance. Would it not be better to discuss terms, equitable terms, at the outset?'

'You're not a betting man, Mr Holmes?' asked Sir George.

'Oh, I'm not averse to the occasional flutter. But I study the odds as well as the form. It strikes me that we are pretty evenly matched, and so we must look at the outsiders, consider their prospects, and the effect of chance, which is, as I say, proverbially blind. Consider, Sir George, and you, too, Sir James. An unexpected setback, a delay of a few minutes in the critical stages, one's cab held up by the traffic, say, might mean the difference between success and failure. Well, Sir George?'

Sir George thought for a long moment before replying. 'I'm a betting man through and through, Mr Holmes. If by some chance I were to solve the puzzle, I'd be half a million to the good. On the other hand, I had no expectations from the late Lord Hammerford, certainly not after my first wife died, so if I don't succeed, why, I've lost nothing.'

'Some would say you had lost a good deal, Sir George,' murmured Holmes.

'Oh, I don't look at things in that way, and never have done. We'll each follow our noses, and the devil take the hindmost,' said Sir George.

'As you wish,' Holmes told him. 'By the way, Sir George, you have not had Sir James here followed, have you?'

'Followed? Why do you say that? No, devil a bit of it!' Sir George leaned forward in his chair, clenching his fists at the enormity of the suggestion.

Holmes raised a hand. 'I intend no offence,' said he. 'But we were certainly followed here from our rooms. And we have reason to believe that Sir James had been followed to our rooms to begin with.'

Sir George subsided, and shook his head. 'No, Mr Holmes, but it's odd you should say that.'

'And why odd, pray?'

'Well, you'll maybe think it a fancy on my part, but I have had the distinct impression that someone has been following me all day, too.'

'Ah! You did not see anyone? Not a little rat-like fellow?'

Sir George shook his head. 'The only fellow who looked at all suspicious was a big chap, a regular bruiser. He seemed to be on my track for a couple of hours, but then I lost him.'

'Holmes!' said I. 'That —'

He shook his head to silence me. 'Two of them, then,' he said, half to himself. 'More than two probably, for the little fellow was with Sir James. Yes, and they change over if suspicions are aroused. And they are acting under orders, or I miss my guess.' He looked at Sir George. 'Would it interest you to learn that there has been an attempt to abduct the young Lord Hammerford?'

'The devil there has?' There was genuine surprise on Sir George's face, or I have never seen it. He seemed about to say more, then shook his head, as if in disbelief.

'Before our very door,' added Holmes calmly. 'Which gives us something of a personal interest in the matter.' He studied Sir George closely before going on, 'I may add that our first, rather uncharitable, thought was that you might be somehow involved.'

Sir George leapt to his feet at this, and I started up from my own chair, ready to go to Holmes's defence. But then Sir George gave a shaky laugh, and subsided once more. 'No need for that nonsense,' he said almost to himself as he sat down. 'It was perhaps a natural enough thought, Mr Holmes, in all conscience, since you don't know me. It does interest me, Mr Holmes, greatly. But I assure you, sir, that I would never get involved in anything of that sordid description. Why, what sort of man would harm a child?'

'A wicked man!' said I.

'A man intent on getting his hands on the late Lord Hammerford's fortune,' said Holmes with no change in his calm demeanour. He gazed at Sir George. 'No, I do not believe you would touch anything of that sort, Sir George.'

Sir George looked at Holmes acutely. 'And who would? If I was your first thought, then may I ask what your second thought was?'

'All in good time,' said Holmes. 'Might I have a moment to study the copy of the will which Sir James gave me earlier? I have not yet read it in detail,' and he took the copy from his pocket and settled down to read it without waiting for any answer.

I took this opportunity to catch Sir James's eye, and he summoned the steward, who provided us with brandy and water, Holmes remaining inert throughout the whole trans-action. At length he looked up from the will. 'H'mm! Yes, Sir James, a brandy would be very pleasant, thank you. The will has been published, I take it?'

Sir James nodded. 'The press reports gave only the barest outline, though,' he said. He coughed delicately. 'I know many of the editors and what have you, and I asked them to play it down somewhat. Suppress the more sensational aspects, leave out some of the more sordid details.'

'But the total amount of the estate was in all the papers?'

'Yes. That could not be kept out.'

'Half a million pounds is itself rather sensational, a figure which commands some attention,' said Holmes. 'It catches the eye, as it were. An unscrupulous man might well think that a couple of shillings to the appropriate authorities to look at the will was money well spent. The will itself mentions the fact that whomsoever finds the money is to keep it, and it further specifies that identical envelopes are left for the present Lord Hammerford and for you, Sir George. Now, that same hypothetical and unscrupulous man might read all that, and then go on to think that it might profit him to have the two recipients of the envelopes followed, just to see where they may lead. If nowhere, well, all that has been lost is a little time and money; but if they, or one of them, should lead to half a million — well, that would indeed be a few pounds well spent, would it not?'

Sir George looked uneasy at all this, and even Sir James's usually untroubled brow clouded just a little.

Holmes went on, 'I may tell you, gentlemen, that there is in London at least one large criminal gang to my knowledge. I myself had the honour to remove from circulation its head, and some of his closest associates, but the gang resembles some of the more revolting creatures of classical mythology. Cut off the head but leave the body intact, and the entire thing will spring up again when you least expect it. And besides that gang, there are others, to say nothing of various enterprising individuals. It would, after all, be galling to lay one's hands on the treasure only to have it grabbed by Bill Sykes with his bludgeon at the last.'

'And you think that this gang made the attempt on the lad, Lord Hammerford, I mean?' asked Sir George.

Holmes nodded. 'That gang, or another.'

'Well,' said Sir George, 'perhaps I spoke rather hastily.' He lowered his head to look at the unopened envelope which lay on his knee, then lifted his eyes to regard Sir James. 'Fifty-fifty?'

Sir James shook his head. 'I fear I can scarcely compromise young Lord Hammerford's interests by any sort of division or disbursement at the start.'

'That's fair enough,' said Sir George. He stood up. 'Thank you for your hospitality, Sir James. Mr Holmes, Doctor, I'm sure we shall run into one another in the not too distant future.' And he nodded a last farewell. 'I'll not open my envelope until I'm outside,' he added, 'but you may do as you choose.'

'There is one further point,' said Holmes.

Sir George sat down again rather abruptly. 'Well, sir?'

'There has been this vicious attempt upon young Lord Hammerford, undoubtedly by the gang of which I spoke, or some competitors in villainy. If we cannot join forces, then at the very least — at the very least, Sir George, and you, Sir James — I urge the greatest caution, for yourselves and those you hold dear.'

Sir George cursed. 'If these villains harm my —' he broke off abruptly, and looked at Sir James. 'No offence, but might I have a private word with Mr Holmes and Doctor Watson?'

Sir James got to his feet. 'Certainly, certainly. I'll go wash my hands.' And he nodded to Holmes and me, and left us alone.

'Now, Sir George?'

Sir George looked a trifle embarrassed, then said, 'It's this way, Mr Holmes. Someone has been buying up — well, buying up my debts.'

'Ah. You are certain?'

Sir George nodded. 'An old friend of mine tipped me the wink yesterday. One of my erstwhile creditors, to be blunt, though my people have dealt with his firm so long they're almost part of the family. A respectable old-established firm, in fact you gentlemen have probably dealt with them yourselves from time to time. Anyway, I'd thought at first that he was after me for a little something on account, but he waved a hand and told me, "Don't worry yourself having to think up an excuse, Sir George, it's not that I'm here for", and he goes on to tell me that he's had a handsome offer, and, since times are hard, he's sold my paper to an unknown buyer, but he trusts we'll still be friends.'

'An unknown buyer?' said Holmes quickly.

'Nobody he knew, Mr Holmes. He'd tell me if he knew who it was, I'm sure of that.'

'So, not someone usually in that line of business, then. Tell me, Sir George, was there much of this paper of yours?'

'A ream or two, if not a whole case,' said Sir George carelessly.

I put in, 'However much the amount, surely this mysterious unknown buyer would have a claim to be reimbursed only to the extent of the debt? It was not as much as half a million, I take it?' I asked Sir George.

'Faith, no! Even I couldn't spend that much in a lifetime! No, Doctor, I wish whoever it is the best of luck with it. Like yourself, I fail to see what their reasoning was.'

'Oh, that is easy enough,' said Holmes. 'They propose to dun you, to make life awkward to the extent that you will compound with them, sign some agreement offering, say, half of any amount you may acquire, in exchange for their writing off your present debts. That would be nothing new, after all.'

'Damn it, I believe you're right! Well, I'll see them —'

'You undoubtedly will see them. But that is not what I fear, Sir George,' said Holmes. 'It may well be that there are two gangs of enterprising villains with different approaches to the problem of separating you from any prospective cash. You were, I think, about to say earlier that you would take a dim view of anyone who threatened your wife?'

Sir George started at this. 'I was, sir. And what of that?'

'Only that I do not think the buyer of your debts is behind the attempt upon young Lord Hammerford, which means that we have to contend with at least two interested parties, so to speak. Your people, these mysterious new creditors, may be relatively civilized in their approach, even though they are a trifle underhand. But if the people behind the kidnap attempt are who I think they are, they will not approach you directly with any threats, to you or to Lady Lewis. That is not their way. They work in secret, in the dark, and they do not scruple to use violent means. They do not play by Lord Queensbury's rules, Sir George. I urge you again to take every precaution for your wife's safety. Have you any men in the house?'

'Not just at the moment,' said Sir George, rattling the loose change in his pocket in a significant fashion.

Holmes looked at me. 'Any ideas, Watson?'

'Well, there is Peterson,' I said. 'A commissionaire of our acquaintance,' I added to Sir George. 'An excellent fellow, and I'm sure he would stay with you for a time, until this matter is resolved one way or the other.'

'I fear I'd not be able to recompense him for his time and trouble, not unless I was the lucky man who found the treasure.'

'H'mm. I'm a touch embarrassed in that department myself just now,' I said.

Holmes made an impatient gesture. 'I shall see to that,' said he. 'You can settle with me whenever it may be convenient, Sir George.'

'It's devilish good of you,' muttered Sir George.

'Not at all. I have as great a distaste for these villains as you. Greater, indeed, for I have an old score to settle with them. Do you have a card? Thank you. And we shall send Peterson round as soon as may be. Now, I think I shall approach Sir James once again, see if we really cannot have an amnesty. Perhaps you would remain here, Sir George? Thank you.' And Holmes went off to rejoin Sir James, who was reading a newspaper at the far side of the room. After a moment, he returned, an angry look on his face. 'I fear that my best efforts have been unable to persuade him,' said he.

'I expected nothing else,' said Sir George. 'And, that being the case, I'll take my leave, with many thanks for your consideration.'

'Very well. But shall we agree to leave the discussions open?' suggested Holmes. 'We may find that pooling our efforts looks more tempting as time goes on.'

Sir George shrugged. 'I'm game if you are. It's Sir James you must convince.' And with that, he took his leave.

When he had gone, Holmes looked angrily at Sir James. 'I can scarcely believe that you have acquired so shining a reputation as a diplomat, Sir James. I would have treated with him,' he said.

'Fifty-fifty? Come, Mr Holmes!'

'A quarter of a million is better than nothing at all, Sir James. And besides, if this Sir George is as desperate for cash as you seem to think, and as he himself suggests, it might not have taken quite that much to ensure his co-operation. A few thousand might be money well spent to safeguard the bulk of the treasure. Although I myself would have opened the bidding at a more modest level, five hundred, shall we say?'

Sir James laughed at this. 'The rascal would never have settled for that.'

'No, but he might have settled for ten times that, which would still have been a modest finder's fee, should one choose to consider it in that light. Now, you must excuse me. I shall be back as soon as may be, and you will please stay here until I return.' And, before either Sir James or I could speak, Holmes was out of his chair and away.

'Well!' said a surprised Sir James, looking at the door. 'And what's he up to, d'you think?'

'I suspect he's following Sir George,' I said. 'I can't imagine what else he'd be doing. You mustn't mind Holmes, Sir James, he ignores some of the conventional pretensions of society, but that's just his way. His methods may not be to everyone's taste, but they get results. By the way, we have a little commission for Peterson, if you are sure the boy will be safe with you.'

'Oh, yes, he'll be safe enough once he's back at my house. In my line of business, I have to make make certain the house is secure, you understand.'

'Of course.'

'So you can have Peterson whenever you want him.' Sir James stretched, and looked at his watch. 'Well, since we're to stay here, what do you say to a spot of lunch? I see the General is stirring, so evidently he feels it must be nearly the hour.'

I agreed readily enough, for the club had an excellent reputation for its food. As we moved to the dining room, Sir James asked me, 'By the way, Watson, what do you think to our Sir George?'

'Headstrong, I should say. But by no means unlikeable, under the right circumstances. A bad enemy, but a good friend, or I miss my guess.'

Sir James nodded. 'So I think, too.'

'He's a good talker,' I added.

'Ah, that's the Irish in him!' said Sir James. He reflected a moment. 'He has a way with him, as my old mother would have said, there's no denying it. Under the right circumstances, we might have been friends. Still, you can't change things that easily.'

We had our lunch, and a couple of cigars. Sir James was a good talker, and we exchanged a few yarns about our military service, our travels, and the like. Still, as time wore on I fear we both became a little restive. Sir James had looked at his watch a dozen times before Holmes eventually strolled into the room as if nothing had happened. 'Ah, Mr Holmes, at last!' said Sir James. 'We were hoping you would return ere long.'

Holmes laughed. 'My apologies, gentlemen,' he said, 'but I had urgent business. However, I am now quite at your disposal.'

Sir James nodded at the envelope which still lay, unopened, upon the table. 'Is it not time we were getting on, Mr Holmes?'

Holmes nodded. 'Before I agree to continue, though, I must insist that you leave any future discussions, whether with Sir George or anyone else, to me.'

Sir James frowned, then nodded. 'Agreed. Now, let us see what the next clue may be.'

Holmes slit open the envelope, and took out the sheet of paper it contained.

FOUR

Sherlock Holmes took out the sheet of paper, and studied it intently for a time before placing it upon the table. I read — 'EMHMNQ OBPSLBEHJ KG KAD KAEDD IDQQDH CBED, JDD QGIHFMJA QGMNQ VT BNH HGLN.'

It was, of course, quite wrong of me, but as so often on these occasions I fear that I could not resist the temptation. 'A code of some sort, perhaps, Holmes?'

'Remarkable, Watson!' he laughed. 'From your alertness of mind no less than your liveliness of demeanour, I venture to deduce a bottle, if not two, of Beaune at lunch. Yes, my boy, a simple transposition, I fancy. What do you make of it?'

'Well, I know that "e" is the most frequent letter, as a rule, and we have seven, no, eight occurrences of the letter "d" here, and no other letter occurs more often, so take that as a first step.' I scratched my head, metaphorically speaking. 'Perhaps I had best leave the rest to you, Holmes.'

He laughed. 'We have "jdd" here, Watson. If your "d" equals "e" is correct, then, despite the tempting theory that there is an apiarist or a golfer involved, the logical word is "see" something or another. H'mm! Unfortunately, "j" does not occur as frequently as one might wish. Still, if we then go on to assume that "kad" is "the", which is a logical assumption for a three-letter group ending in "e", then where does that take us?' He produced a piece of paper and a pencil, and began scribbling away.

Fired by Holmes's enthusiasm, I picked up a piece of paper myself. 'If "k" is "t", "a" is "h" and "d" is "e", then "e" must be "r", surely? The fifth word must be "three" something,' I pointed out. 'And "kg" must be "to", if "kad" is "the", for nothing else makes sense.'

'Well done!' Yes, so let us take as a first theory that "a" in the code is "h", and "d" is "e", "e" is "r", "g" is "o" —'

'"Hero"! Oh, no, for there are some gaps.'

'But not so many as to be inexplicable,' said Holmes in a kindly tone. 'Try "Hammerford", Watson.' He scribbled away again, frowned, then laughed. 'Yes, his own name, "Hammerford", ignoring any duplication of the letters, then "last will and —" and "testament" would come next, of course, only the letters had all been used. Then, I fancy, the rest of the alphabet in its regular order, although that is less important. Only instead of using "h" for "a", as you or I might have done, he has reversed it, so to speak, used the regular alphabet as the code, if I make it clear.'

He did not, but I had the gist of it, and you can readily imagine that I would not give him the satisfaction of explaining further. 'Oh, absolutely. As crystal, Holmes.'

Sir James, who had been looking on in some evident bewilderment, cleared his throat. 'You are, of course, used to this sort of thing, Mr Holmes, and Doctor Watson here is clearly not much less expert than yourself, but I am afraid —'

'Ah. I beg your pardon, Sir James. Lord Hammerford wrote down his own name, "Hammerford", then the phrase "last will and testament", which seemed appropriate to him under the circumstances. Then those letters, in their order, correspond to the letters of the conventional "abc". Some letters occur twice, but duplication is simply ignored. Then the rest of the alphabet follows in its normal order. You follow?'

'Not entirely, but I am sure that you are correct,' Sir James told him.

Holmes frowned at his piece of paper.

'Well?' asked Sir James.

'Well, I fear that after all that, it does not immediately mean a great deal.' Holmes passed the sheet to me.

'"Riding backwards to the three-legged mare, see goldfish going up and down",' I read aloud. 'Oh, well, Holmes, the best of us can make the occasional mistake. Just have to think again, won't we?'

He shook his head impatiently. 'There is no mistake, Watson. Why, you yourself derived much of the code. No, my boy, this is another little puzzle for us.'

I frowned. 'The "three-legged mare" was the gallows at Tyburn, of course,' I ventured. 'And criminals condemned to hang were driven there seated backwards. Popular superstition claims that it was to add to the ignominy, but most authorities agree that in actual fact it was done that way so that the sight of the gallows might not unnerve them too much, so that they caused no fuss towards the end.'

'A most interesting aside on criminal history, Watson. More to our immediate purpose, the processional route led up Holborn, if memory serves me correctly?'

'It does, Holmes. We are to look in Holborn, then, for these — goldfish, was it?'

'Yes, and going up and down. H'mm.'

'I cannot recall any suppliers of tropical fish in Holborn,' said I, doubtfully. 'What about a taxidermist, though?'

'Even the most enthusiastic and dedicated of anglers would scarcely have a goldfish stuffed and set in a case!' said Holmes, laughing. 'No, my boy, a supplier of aquaria is, as you say, the likely meaning, but I cannot recollect seeing such a shop there either. H'mm. Perhaps one of the side roads is meant? Anyway, we have our location, so it might be as well to take a stroll up Holborn, and see what we may see.'

That we did, and in the most literal sense possible. We strolled from St Paul's up Newgate Street, Holborn Viaduct, Holborn Circus, Holborn, High Holborn, St Giles, Oxford Street, to Marble Arch. And down. And up again, with an increasing confusion and frustration that eventually came close to despair.

By the time we had made our third circuit it was getting towards the hour of dinner, and still none of us had the slightest idea as to where we should look next. There was no sign of any shop selling aquarium supplies, or anything of that kind, no hint of a goldfish. We did find a seller of singing canaries, and so desperate were we that we even enquired there. 'Goldfish?' said the owner, puzzled. 'No, sorry, gents. I can get you one, though, if you'd like?'

Personally, I was growing increasingly convinced that Holmes had simply read the code wrongly, and hinted as much more than once, but the thunderous expression on his face prevented my elaborating upon this theory. Whether the reading of the code were right or wrong, Holmes was none the less at as much of a loss as I was myself. I had some fears that he was about to suggest a fourth perambulation of the road, but he caught the look in my eye, and laughed aloud. 'No, Watson,' he told me, shaking his head, 'I scarcely think that another walk will tell us more than we have learned already.'

'Which is precisely nothing.'

'I would not say that. We have added to our knowledge of London, have we not? And the more alert members of our little group cannot have failed to notice that Sir George Lewis has been keeping a close eye on us from handy doorways and similar lurking spots.'

'Has he? I had not seen him,' I exclaimed.

'Perhaps not, but he is there,' said Holmes. 'It is interesting, and perhaps also instructive, for if he had any more idea than we ourselves have, he would surely have gone straight to the position indicated. Indeed, I rather suspect that he has not actually solved the code, but that he is simply following us.'

'And this mysterious gang of yours? Are they here too?' I asked, with some disbelief.

'Oh, yes. There is one of them not a dozen yards behind us now, another on the far side of the road, though I suspect that one is shadowing Sir George. They must be even more puzzled than we are!' he added with a laugh. He stretched. 'Well, gentlemen, you may have lunched heartily, but I ate nothing, so if you are agreeable, I suggest we leave it for today, and investigate what Mrs Hudson has prepared for dinner. Who knows, the answer may come if we sleep on it?' His words were light-hearted enough, and his tone matched them, but I could tell he was bitterly disappointed with our lack of success.

Sir James refused Holmes's suggestion that we should dine together, saying that it would be as well to ensure that all was well with young Lord Hammerford, following the day's excitement. 'Very well,' Holmes told him, 'but I must repeat my injunction that you exercise the greatest care not only for the safety of the boy but also that of the rest of your family, including yourself.'

Sir James nodded. 'I'll do that, you may be sure. Well, gentlemen, I'll take my leave now, and call upon you again tomorrow, if that's satisfactory.' We saw him safely into a cab, and walked back to Baker Street.

Our ancestors were wont to refer to one who had been flogged at the cart's tail as having had 'air and exercise,' and my own air and exercise in our tracing of the condemned felon's route back and forth had given me an excellent appetite for my dinner. But Holmes, despite his remarks as to having missed his lunch, did no more than toy with his food. I remonstrated with him, but all in vain, and before I had half finished my own meal he had risen from the table with a mumbled apology, lit his pipe, and started to examine the coded message again. 'It is right!' he muttered, more than once, 'It is right, and yet it makes no sort of sense.' He was still at it when I said good night and went to bed.

When I came down to breakfast next morning, Holmes was still sitting in his armchair, looking for all the world as if he had never moved all night. 'Have you been to bed, Holmes?' I demanded angrily.

He dismissed this ridiculous suggestion with a wave of the hand. 'There are three possibilities,' he told me. 'First, the clue refers to some temporary object or phenomenon, which we could not find because it is no longer there.'

'Improbable,' I said, handing him a full plate. 'Old Lord Hammerford could not know just when he would die and the will would be read. It must be of a more permanent nature.'

Holmes nodded, and began to tackle the food before him. 'Quite right. Well, then, second, the clue is so very obscure that we have not yet been able to solve it. That is surely the true explanation.' And he poured himself coffee, and began to eat in earnest, to my great delight, for he often starves himself too much for his own good when engaged on a case.

'And your third possibility?' I enquired after a reasonable interval.

He waved his hand again. 'Oh, that we have indeed made a mistake with the code, but I discount that.'

'"We" have made a mistake?'

Holmes laughed, and stood up. 'That was an excellent breakfast,' he said. 'I think I shall take my doctor's advice, and have a couple of hours' sleep. The answer may come unbidden to the rested mind.' And off he went to his room.

I was now at something of a loose end myself. I glanced at the great heap of rough notes and jottings which Holmes had produced in his efforts to find an alternative reading of the code, but could make little of them, beyond the fact that our original interpretation had been correct. 'Goldfish going up and down, indeed!' I muttered to myself. And I echoed Holmes's own comment, 'Makes no sense at all.' I gave it up, and decided to take a walk to try to clear my head.

My footsteps took me involuntarily towards Oxford Street, and the memory of last night's five or six miles' fruitless walking made me shudder. I hastily crossed the road, and determined to spend the rest of the morning in my club, which is not so large, or so grand, as the one which we had visited on the previous day, but none the less it suits me.

The club was pretty well deserted at that ungodly hour, but on entering the smoking room about the first man I set eyes upon was old Thurston. I was pleased to see him, for Thurston is one of the few men, apart from Holmes, with whom I can claim any sort of friendship. If he has a fault, it is that he is forever trying to make his fortune by speculating in all kinds of strange ventures. He once tried to induce me to go into partnership with him to buy a farm in South Africa, but I thought better of it. Thurston bore me no ill-will for that refusal, saying merely that 'It was probably just as well, for we'd have failed at it.' More to my immediate purpose, he has a vast fund of knowledge and stories about the world in general, and London in particular. Indeed, it was Thurston who told me an interesting and most amusing fact about Nelson's Column, which unfortunately I cannot set down in a publication intended for the general reader. I hailed him, therefore, with some delight, and lost no time in asking what he knew about goldfish.

Thurston shook his head. 'You mean those sort of tropical whitebait things? Can't say I know anything, old boy. Oh, they give them away as prizes at fairs. I know that because my nephews are forever taking them home. Drives my sister mad, because the damned things die almost immediately. Still, keeps the cat happy, doesn't it?'

'I suppose so.' I tried one last time. 'So, if I were to ask you whereabouts in London I could see goldfish going up and down, I suppose you'd have no idea?'

'Holborn, old chap. The "Queen Victoria" there.'

'The what? Pub, is it? I didn't notice —'

Thurston shook his head. 'New gentlemen's convenience. I don't really mean "new gentlemen", of course, but rather a new convenience for the — ah, well, the convenience of gentlemen,' he explained. 'Been built a couple of years, now.'

'You're pulling my leg?'

Thurston shook his head. 'Fact. 'Ninety-eight, if I remember correctly.'

'No, I mean about the goldfish. And why "Queen Victoria", pray?'

'Oh, I see what you mean. I don't know why they call 'em "Queen Victorias", unless it refers to the Act which established them early on in her reign. Better than some names I've heard for them, of course.'

'And the goldfish, man?' I snarled.

'No, that's a fact, too. The — what d'you call 'em? The cisterns, that's it, they have glass sides, and the chap who looks after the place thought they look like fish tanks, which is quite right, they do, and so he had the rather odd notion of putting goldfish in 'em! Of course, every time the things are flushed, the poor fish go down in the world, until the tide rises again! Ever hear of such a thing? Mind you, I recall one time in Buda-Pesth —'

But I fear that his tale, interesting though I had no doubt it would be, had to wait, for I was already on my feet and halfway to the door. 'Thanks,' I called back to him, 'I'll buy you a drink next time I see you. Got to rush now.'

I fairly ran to Holborn, and quickly found the edifice which Thurston had mentioned. I could not, of course, know just what dispositions the late Lord Hammerford had made for the safe-keeping and collection of the next clue, but I had no doubt that it would be similar to the arrangement at his club. Accordingly, I wandered into the place as if there on business. An elderly gentleman, evidently under some degree of strain, brushed past me as I hesitated in the entrance. 'Going in, or not?' he demanded.

'If you must know, sir, I have come to look at the gold-fish,' I told him, feeling rather foolish.

'Well, as long as that's all you want to gawp at.'

'Really, sir!'

The attendant, who had evidently overheard this exchange, walked up to me. 'Lots of gentlemen come to look at my fish, by personal recommendation, as it were, sir,' he told me.

'Indeed? I was told of them by a friend, just as you say, but I confess I half thought he was joking.'

'No joke, sir.' The fellow waved towards the ceiling, and I saw that the glass-sided tanks were indeed full of goldfish. 'Remarkable!' I said, and handed him a couple of shillings. 'They must be good for business.'

He laughed. 'Quite a tourist attraction, as you might say, sir. It's just a pity the ladies can't see them.'

'Indeed.' I glanced round. 'Tell me, you don't happen to recall a certain Lord Hammerford coming here to admire the fish?'

His expression changed. 'Lord Hammerford, sir?' he asked woodenly.

'Yes. I have an idea he may possibly have left something with you, to be called for.'

His good humour returned at once. 'This way, sir, if you

please.' He led me into a little room away from the main current of humanity that thronged the place. It was as comfortably furnished as many a bachelor's flat that I have seen. 'If you'll wait a moment, sir,' and he disappeared, leaving me to admire the decor. A moment later he returned, bearing the now familiar envelope.

'Ah, that's it,' said I, handing him a sovereign.

'Thank you, sir. Though that's been taken care of, as you might say. Well, sir, if that's all? I have to get back to my work.'

I thanked him again, and turned to go. Then I stopped, and did some thinking. It was not outside the bounds of possibility that I had been followed here, although the place was one which I might have visited for innocent enough reasons. Having done rather well, or so I flattered myself, it would be idiotic of me to lose this valuable clue by inattention to detail. Accordingly, I removed my hat and lodged the envelope securely therein. I returned my hat to my head, then took from my pocketbook an envelope of broadly similar appearance which happened to be in there, and with this second envelope clutched firmly in my hand, I emerged once more into the daylight.

I do not think that Holmes himself could have reasoned more acutely, or taken better precautions. That those precautions were justified was proved almost immediately I stepped into the street, blinking at the sunlight after the cool, dark marble interior I had just left. That same large rough whom I had encountered earlier, who was now well on his way to becoming an old acquaintance, suddenly sprang at me from the stream of passers-by, knocked me down, snatched the envelope from my unresisting hand,

and made off down the street. A few of the pedestrians gazed curiously at this little drama, but in the way of a London crowd there was little general movement either to help me to my feet or to pursue my attacker.

One man, though, did bend over me and offer his hand. 'A little trouble, eh, Doctor?' I recognized the cynical tones of Sir George Lewis.

'Oh, nothing serious. Thank you, Sir George,' I said as I got to my feet and dusted myself down.

'Take anything valuable, did he?' Sir George asked with a nod down the road in the direction in which my assailant had vanished. 'Seemed to me to snatch an envelope, or something of that kind.'

'Not at all. It was merely a tailor's bill which I had been intending to pay some time.'

Sir George threw back his head and laughed, to the astonishment of several ladies and gentlemen on the pavement. 'It's the devil himself would be needing a long spoon to sup with Doctor Watson!' said he. 'So, it was nothing more than that, was it? For a moment, you know, I thought you might have found the next clue back there,' and he nodded to the temple of Cloacina from which I had recently emerged.

'Not a bit of it,' I said, with what conviction I could manage.

'H'mm. Well, you'll not be offended if I take a look in there myself?' Before I could answer, he had entered the building, to emerge in triumph a moment later. 'Very interesting fish,' he said. 'Was that what that code nonsense was all about, then? Damned if I'd ever have solved it. I'm just pleased I decided to follow you!'

I should have been angry at this, but I found I could not. Despite the fact that Sir George was, for the moment at least, the rival, perhaps even the enemy, of Holmes, and thus of myself, I could not dislike the man. 'But why me?' I asked. 'Holmes would have been a better bet.'

'Ah, but he didn't shift from the house. Though I thought at first that it might be an elaborate hoax. Still, better to be born lucky than rich, eh?'

'Well, we're even,' I said with a laugh. 'I owe you my thanks for your helping hand, and you owe me yours for the clue.' As he had done earlier, I looked down the road which my assailant had taken. 'Look here, Sir George, that fellow had evidently followed me, and I have no doubt that you, too, are being shadowed at the moment. Things seem to be hotting up a bit too much for my taste, I confess. We may both of us be in considerable danger at the moment, particularly when these rogues discover my substitution trick. What do you say to a temporary truce, at least until we reach the cab-stand and can get safely to our respective homes?'

'I'd be all for it,' said he, 'but I'll not be taking a cab today,' and he tapped his pockets as if to indicate that they were empty.

'Oh, as to that,' I said, 'I can manage a small loan,' and I handed him a few shillings. 'Pay me back when you can.'

'I'm exceedingly grateful,' he said, embarrassed. 'I'll repay you when this is all over, eh? We'll sit down and have a drink, and a cigar.'

'And a laugh about all our misadventures?'

'Well,' said Sir George with a grin, 'whoever finds the dibs will be laughing, I have no doubt!'

'By the by, how is Peterson?'

'Oh, he's settled in. I'm very grateful to Mr Holmes, and of course to you, Doctor.' Sir George seemed positively embarrassed.

'Think nothing of it,' I told him. 'We may be thrown into a sort of passing rivalry by this nonsense over the will, but there's no animosity in it. Merely a professional case for us. And even if it were not so, we could not and would not permit these ruffians to threaten women and children.'

Sir George stopped, turned to me, and shook my hand vigorously without speaking. We found a couple of cabs, and went our separate ways without more ado.

Sir James's carriage was standing at our door when I got back to Baker Street, and the coachman, who was now becoming something of a regular acquaintance, just like the rough, gave me a cynical smile as he touched his hat. When I reached the sitting room, I found Holmes was poring once more over his bits of paper, while Sir James sat silent and morose in a corner, smoking a cigar.

'No luck, eh?' I asked sympathetically.

'I fear not. I can really see no hope for it but to walk the route yet again, and hope that something suggests itself. Indeed,' he added with a hint of reprobation, 'we have been awaiting your return so that we might go together.'

'Oh, I don't know that I can be bothered,' I said with an exaggerated yawn. The other two stared at me in some astonishment. I went on, 'It really does not strike me as worthwhile, all this chasing about. Still, if you do find the answer, it might be as well to keep it under your hat,' and I laid my hat upside down on the table before Holmes.

Holmes continued to look at me in astonishment for a

moment, then he looked at my hat, then finally he picked the hat up and took the envelope from inside it. 'How on earth did you find this, Watson?' he asked admiringly.,

'It's a rather curious story, Holmes —'

'Never mind, the important thing is you have it. Well done, Watson!' and he ripped the envelope open.

FIVE

'You have really surpassed yourself this time, Watson,' said Holmes as he opened the envelope. 'You must tell us the whole story, but not just at the moment, for time is of the essence. The thing now is to continue the hunt. Do you know if Sir George has also found this particular clue?'

'I fear he has.'

'H'mm. Well, let us see what we have.' He read the paper, then handed it to me.

'"The keeper of the graven images holds what you seek". Sounds almost biblical, Holmes.'

'I fancy it may be quite near at hand, though. Just round the corner, in fact.'

'Oh?'

'Why, Madame Tussaud's, of course.' Holmes stood up, and sought his coat and hat.

'You know, Holmes,' I said as we walked along Baker Street, 'one flaw in this whole scheme of old Lord Hammerford's has struck me.'

'And what might that be?'

'It is all so very dependent upon the goodwill of individuals. The attendant at the club, another at the — the place where I found this last clue, and presumably yet another whither we now going. Suppose that any one of these various men had died, or moved away? We should never have found the clue they once held. Or suppose that they had grown curious as to what had been entrusted to them? Any one of them might have opened the envelopes, searched for the treasure, and simply denied any knowledge of old Lord Hammerford.'

Holmes shook his head. 'You raise some very interesting points, but I think I can answer them. Old Lord Hammerford would not have told them what the envelopes meant, of course, but simply asked them to be kept until called for. Those entrusted with the clues would thus not know that Lord Hammerford himself would not return to collect them, and so they would not dare to open them, or otherwise tamper with them. There was a slight danger, I allow, that they might be tempted to pry once they heard the news of old Lord Hammerford's death, but then they would surely imagine that the solicitors, or heirs, would enquire after the envelopes — as is indeed the case. Besides, what would a blank sheet of paper, or a curious code, mean to a casual reader? Without the background history, it is meaningless. I presume that they were well paid to be faithful, perhaps they even received a regular fee; whereas on the other hand they had little or nothing to gain by betraying Lord Hammerford's trust. But there is another point, closely allied to yours, which does cause me concern.'

'And that is?'

'That the gang which I fear might somehow intimidate or bribe one of the guardians of the clues, and put up an obstacle that way. Or Sir George himself might do something along those lines.'

'I hardly think a gentleman would act in such a fashion,

Holmes.'

'Possibly not, under normal circumstances, but half a million might overcome a good many gentlemanly scruples.' He frowned. 'And now that I come to think of it, I may have dismissed your other suggestions too lightly. Now that the will has been published, the thought of this vast fortune may arouse idle curiosity and might weaken even an honest servant's resolve. In that instance it is less their solving the riddles that I fear, but more the fact that they might destroy or withhold them, so they are lost to us.' And his stride lengthened at the thought.

Madame Tussaud's world-famous establishment is, of course, at no great distance from our rooms in 221B, and in a couple of minutes we were there, to find the usual horde of trippers thronged around the entrance. Holmes showed a touch of impatience, and when the crowd had thinned out temporarily, he approached the attendant.

'Shilling each, sixpence extra for the Chamber of 'Orrors and the relics of Napoleon,' said the man.

'Ah, no, you misunderstand. We do not wish to see the exhibits,' said Holmes. He took out a half-sovereign, and weighed it in his hand. 'I believe you have a message of some sort, an envelope, perhaps, to be called for, by friends of Lord Hammerford? We should be most grateful —'

'I'm sure you would, but I haven't the least notion of what you're talking about.' Had there not been a window between them, I am sure that the fellow would have shoved Holmes aside bodily to allow the next batch of sightseers access to the show.

'H'mm. This is not what I was expecting,' said Holmes, springing nimbly aside as a large lady prodded him in the ribs with her umbrella by way of encouraging him to relocate himself. 'No need to push, madam, I shall happily get out of your way as soon as I can.'

'What did I tell you?' I asked, as we moved out of the stream. 'This fellow has been somehow enticed or bullied into betraying his trust.'

Holmes shook his head. 'If he is dissembling, then he is a very good actor,' he told me. He waited again until the rush had fallen off somewhat, then approached the man again, this time with a whole sovereign prominently displayed. 'Perhaps I phrased my question badly,' Holmes began, 'but are you sure the name "Hammerford" really means nothing to you?'

'I wish it did, sir,' said the man, eyeing the little glittering disc, 'but you see, I've only been in this job a couple of days, so I'm just learning the ropes, as you might say.'

'Ah!' Holmes handed the coin over the counter. 'What was the name of the man who had the post before you, do you know?'

'Can't say as I do, sir. He'd gone, you see, when I started.'

'Retired, was it? Or —?'

'No, sir, retired. The manager would be able to tell you more, if you was to ask him. In the office, sir, down the corridor there.'

'Thank you.' Holmes led the way down a short corridor, and tapped at the door labelled 'Manager'.

'Yes?' came from within.

Holmes opened the door and led us inside. The manager, a short, dark man, rose from his desk as we entered, and looked a question at Holmes.

'My name is Sherlock Homes, this is Doctor Watson,

and Sir James Damery.'

'Indeed? I have heard your name, of course, Mr Holmes. And you, Doctor. And Sir James! You honour me, gentlemen. Please, sit down, and tell me how I may be of service. You are not here,' he glanced round and lowered his voice, 'officially, as it were?'

'We shall not disturb you,' said Holmes. 'We are engaged upon a small investigation, and you are in a position to assist us greatly, if you will.'

'Of course, of course! Anything, Mr Holmes. You have but to name it.'

'We are looking for the gentleman who worked in the ticket office until quite recently.'

'Oh.' The manager seemed disappointed that it was so simple, but soon recovered his composure. 'His name was Wetherspoon,' he said. 'Nice old chap. He retired a week or so back. I have his address here,' and he rummaged amongst some papers, found what he sought, and gave us the address, which proved to be in Bow. Holmes thanked him, and we made our way into the street.

'No need of a cab, we can take my carriage,' said Sir James, and we headed back to our rooms, and were very soon on our way, going towards the East End.

As the carriage moved along at a smart pace, I could not help telling Holmes, 'This rather seems to vindicate my theory, does it not? Of course, if old Lord Hammerford had still been alive, he could simply have made new arrangements with the new man, but as it was, the previous ticket man could not possibly know what should be done with the letters entrusted to him.'

'H'mm. You may well be right,' said Holmes, who always

hated to acknowledge that he was wrong.

Feeling considerably more complacent than was good for my soul, I sank back in my seat and maintained a self-satisfied silence for the remainder of the short journey.

We pulled up in an ordinary enough street at no great distance from Victoria Park, and Holmes knocked upon the door of a house which was no different from any of its neighbours. After a lengthy interval, the door was opened by an elderly man in his shirt sleeves.

'Mr Wetherspoon?' asked Holmes.

'That I am, sir.'

'You worked until quite recently in the ticket office at Madame Tussaud's, I believe?'

'I did, sir. Nothing wrong, is there?' he asked anxiously.

'No, no, nothing of that kind,' said Holmes. He took yet another half-sovereign from his waistcoat pocket, and toyed idly with it. 'I merely wished to ask if the name "Lord Hammerford" meant anything to you?'

Old Mr Wetherspoon frowned. 'Can't say as I recollect the name, sir,' he said at last, with some disappointment in his voice.

'No-one ever left anything with you, to be called for? A couple of envelopes, or anything of that sort?'

Mr Wetherspoon shook his head. 'Folk sometimes asked me to give a message to someone they expected to meet, and that kind of thing, of course. But never envelopes, sir, no.'

'I see. Well, thank you for your trouble, and I'm sorry to have disturbed you like this.' Holmes handed the coin over, but I could tell he was nonplussed.

As the door closed, I said, 'You think he is telling the

truth, Holmes?'

'I fancy he is, Watson. Indeed, I suspect that we have simply misunderstood the riddle.'

'"We", Holmes?'

He laughed, then glanced at the bit of paper again. 'It does say "graven" images and not "waxen" ones,' he mused doubtfully.

'But where in London can one find graven images, Holmes?'

'It is a puzzle, I know, but then I do not imagine that we are actually expected to search for idols of Baal, or anything of that sort. Perhaps a statue might be indicated, though?'

'Too public, surely, Holmes? And besides, statues don't have keepers, do they? Pity there's not another wax museum besides this one.'

'And why do you say that?' asked Holmes.

'Well, we could have tried there.'

'No, why did you think along those lines?'

'For that matter, why did you, when you thought it was Madame Tussaud's?'

Holmes frowned. 'Well, it must be a public place, yet not too public, as we have already determined. And there must be a keeper of some sort. So the logical place is an exhibition, a place of entertainment, that sort of thing. A museum, perhaps? Are there Roman remains in any museum, I wonder?'

'Wait, though, Holmes,' I told him. 'There is another place of entertainment, not too far away — the Egyptian Hall in Piccadilly! That has graven images all right, pharoahs, or mummies or sphinxes, or whatever they are, plastered all over the front.'

'Excellent, Watson!'

'I told you it was biblical,' I said triumphantly.

'Pagan, surely?' queried Sir James, who had listened with some interest.

'I'm sure there was a mention of Egypt in the Bible,' I said, struggling to recall my Sunday school lessons. 'Didn't Moses part the Red Sea to get away from there?'

'Oh, I can believe that,' said Sir James, laughing. 'All that sand, and the heat.'

'Some interesting ruins, though, and some excellent hunting,' said I. 'Never been there myself, of course, but I once met a chap called Blenkinsop, Major Blenkinsop, "Barmy" Blenkinsop we called him. Met him in Quetta, under rather odd circumstances, which I must tell you about some time. Anyway, old "Barmy" was in the Fayum in 'seventy-three, or maybe 'seventy-four —'

'Again, although it has every promise of being most diverting, this will simply have to wait, Watson,' Holmes told me with a hint of impatience. He climbed into the carriage, and we followed, and very soon we were on our way through the City.

'Your theory, though interesting, was not entirely correct, you see, Watson,' said Holmes mischievously as we rattled along. 'Still, you did redeem yourself rather satisfyingly.'

'It is just a pity that I did not think of the Egyptian Hall earlier,' I said, 'for we might have saved some considerable time.'

'Oh, that is nothing, At least you saw the answer, while I have been chasing wild geese,' said Holmes generously.

A very few minutes more, and we were in Piccadilly, and drawing up before Messrs Maskelyne and Cooke's renowned palace of entertainment.

'Graven images, Holmes,' I said, indicating the ornate statuary with which every square foot of the edifice was decorated.

'Indeed.' Holmes pointed with his stick, and I looked, to see Sir George Lewis strolling down the street. 'He had evidently had the same idea as we ourselves,' said Holmes. 'I wonder if he is a happy man just now, or a disappointed one? Well, we shall soon see.' And once again he made his way to the box-office window, and rapped upon it.

After some considerable time, he rapped again, and a surly-looking man appeared. 'Box-office is closed now,' he told us, and turned as if to go back to his luncheon, or whatever we had interrupted.

'One moment, my good man,' said Holmes, tapping a half-sovereign significantly upon the counter.

The man returned, reluctantly as it seemed to me. 'Well?'

Holmes placed the coin down on the little counter, but kept his finger on it. 'I suspect that you may have something for us,' he said. 'We are friends of Lord Hammerford.'

'And 'oo's he, then?'

'Well, then,' said Holmes, 'if the name is unfamiliar, I must ask what did you give Sir George Lewis just now?'

'Who?'

'The gentleman who just called here,' said Holmes sweetly. 'If you lean out of your window, you can just see him turning the corner there.'

'Never seen 'im, never 'eard of 'im. Never heard of any of 'em,' said the attendant. Before Holmes could continue, the fellow pulled down a blind of sorts, and — presumably — made his exit hidden from our gaze.

Holmes turned from the window in some annoyance. 'Well, I suspect he is lying,' he told us.

'He may know nothing of it,' I said. 'You thought the other fellow was ignorant of the whole thing. We may simply have to think again.'

Holmes shook his head. 'The attitude of this man is quite different from that of the wax-museum attendant,' he told me. 'Someone has got to him, or he is acting independently. H'mm. Now, if it is a third party, so to speak, the question is, was it Sir George, or someone else?' And before Sir James or I could venture on any reply to this, Holmes had turned and was off at top speed in the same direction as that in which Sir George had vanished. 'Come along!' he called back to us over his shoulder. 'He has a good start on us, and we must not lose him now.'

Sir James threw me a rueful glance, and we set off after the speeding Holmes. The folk on the pavement stared at us as we scurried along, but Holmes took not the slightest notice. He turned into Savile Row, as Sir George had done, and came to an abrupt halt after a yard or two. I glanced ahead, and saw Sir George himself, standing in front of a fashionable tailor's shop, and lighting a cigar with not the least appearance of haste or concern. He looked at us in some surprise as we neared him. 'Gentlemen,' said he, with a nod. 'We do rather keep on bumping into one another, don't we?'

'As I predicted,' said Holmes calmly, 'which is why I suggested our joining forces, a suggestion I reiterate now. But that is by the way. Sir George, have you found the next clue?'

'Now, how would I know that, without knowing how many clues you may have found?' Sir George's tone was mocking.

'You know quite well what I mean,' said Holmes, annoyed. 'The clue that was left at the Egyptian Hall.'

'Wouldn't know the first thing about it, Mr Holmes, I assure you. Now, if you'll excuse me, my tailor is expecting me.'

'Let me teach him some manners, Holmes,' I said, lifting my stick.

'Now, now, Doctor!' said Sir George. 'You're a good chap, but I'll not stand idle whilst anyone attacks me. And besides,' he added with a grin, 'who's to say that I haven't destroyed both envelopes, after committing the clue to memory? Break my head and you might drive the clue out of it altogether. Amnesia, do you medical men call it?' And he raised his hat to me in an ironic gesture, before entering the tailor's shop.

'Shall I go after him, Holmes?' I asked. 'Say the word and I'll break his head right enough!'

'My dear fellow! In one of the best tailor's in London? That will hardly be necessary, Watson.' Holmes bent down and picked up some fragments of black ash. 'I told you that Sir George had a good start on us. A good enough start to mean that he should have gone further,' he said. 'It is pretty clear that he has been standing here some time, and this, I suspect, is the consequence. It is not cigar ash, note, but rather burnt paper.'

'So the wretch has burned the clues, Holmes!' I exclaimed. 'What on earth can we do now? If he refuses to tell us — well! We could follow him, I suppose,' I added, with something of an anti-climax.

Holmes shook his head. 'He will be on his guard, you may be sure. Watson, Sir James, you both stay here, and if Sir George should emerge, follow him and make sure he sees you following. But I do not think he will emerge, so long as he sees that you are still out here.' And before we could say anything, he nodded a farewell and set off back the way we had come.

Sir James raised an eyebrow. 'Mr Holmes certainly has his own rather odd little ways of approaching a problem,' he said with a smile.

'He has, but I have seen those odd little ways produce the desired result on enough occasions to be confident,' I told him.

We did as Holmes required of us. For half an hour we loitered before the tailor's shop, and I confess that I felt rather foolish. As Holmes had predicted, Sir George made no move to emerge into the street. Sir James made the occasional caustic remark, which I tried to counter as best as I could. At the end of that half hour, I was considerably relieved to see Holmes approaching, with a couple of raga-muffin boys trailing behind him. 'Ah,' I told Sir James, 'I see what Holmes is up to. He has drafted in the irregulars.'

Sir James raised an eyebrow in query, but before I could explain further, Holmes had joined us. The little urchins moved idly to the far side of the road, kicking up the dust and exchanging some lively remarks as they went.

'We may leave safely now, I think,' said Holmes. 'They will mark Sir George and never lose him, wherever he may travel.'

'But won't he spot them?' I asked.

Holmes shrugged. 'I have hopes that he will not. But if he does, then he will not dare to try to obtain the next clue, and that will mean he has no advantage.'

'But nor do we,' I felt obliged to point out. 'It is all very well to prevent Sir George getting to the next clue, but it hardly advances our own search.'

'The idea had occurred to me,' said Holmes drily. 'But we are at something of an impasse, and I confess I see no easy way out. If he does not see us, Sir George may well be inclined to take his chances. If not, if he simply sits tight, then we must think again, of course, but at least he will not lay his hands on the treasure, and that must be our consolation.' He studied his watch. 'Sir James, will you join us for a modest luncheon at 221B?'

Sir James agreed, and we made our way back to Baker Street. Holmes possesses in a quite remarkable degree the ability to shift the focus of his mind, and he entirely refused to discuss the problem immediately before us, saying that there was nothing that we could do until such time as the irregular forces should report that Sir George had made a move. Sir James and I had to be content with this, and the conversation moved over a whole range of subjects in a desultory and disjointed fashion.

Luncheon over, Sir James looked at his watch with just the slightest hint of impatience. 'If you will excuse me, I really should be getting on,' he said. 'Unless, that is, you think there may be some developments, Mr Holmes?'

'As I said earlier, Sir James, we must await Sir George's pleasure,' said Holmes, rising from his chair. 'I shall see you out.'

Before he could do so, however, there was a ring at the

street door. Holmes cocked his head on one side at the sound. 'I wonder if that is one of my delegated watchers, come to report?' he mused, as the steps of the pageboy and the visitor ascended our stairs.

To our very great surprise, though, it was not one of the irregulars whom Billy announced. It was Lady Lewis, the wife of Sir George.

SIX

'Lady Lewis, this is a most unexpected pleasure.' Sir James, who had some acquaintance with the lady, was obviously taken aback at this meeting, but he very quickly recovered his composure and made the necessary introductions.

'Delighted,' said I, and meant it. Lady Lewis was around thirty years of age, strikingly beautiful, with a marvellous head of chestnut-coloured hair. I could quite see why the recently bereaved Sir George had lost no time in marrying her. She was dressed in the fashion, but the fashion of a couple of years earlier, subtly amended by the skilful use of a needle and thread; a suspicion of shininess at the elbows of her jacket, and a hint of darning at the collar, were further indications that the housekeeping budget was not overflowing.

Holmes, ever immune to feminine charms, said merely, 'It is, as Sir James says, a pleasure to meet you, Lady Lewis. But, as he also says, it is most unexpected. You will, I am sure, excuse me one moment,' and he darted to the window and looked out into the street.

Lady Lewis looked at him in some astonishment, but Holmes did not move from the window for a full two minutes, after which he returned to the centre of the room, and remarked, 'It is just as I thought. You have been followed here, Lady Lewis. I trust you did not come here alone?'

'Followed, Mr Holmes? Are you sure? I had no idea that such was the case. Indeed, I feel you must be quite mistaken there.'

Holmes shook his head. 'There is no possibility of error, I assure you. I ask again, did you come here alone?'

'No, Mr Holmes, George — my husband — is quite insistent that I should not leave the house unaccompanied, so I brought Mr Peterson along with me. He is in your kitchen at this very moment.'

'That is excellent in its own way,' said Holmes, 'though I could wish that your escort were rather more substantial. Still, you are safe enough for the time being, so perhaps you could tell us what brings you here?'

Lady Lewis hesitated, and glanced at Sir James without speaking. Sir James, diplomatic as always, said, 'I was just about to leave, madam, so with your permission I shall do so, unless I may be of any service.' And when Lady Lewis shook her head, he suited his action to the words.

'Now, madam,' said Holmes in his most soothing voice, 'we have just had luncheon, but if you would care for some tea? Some light refreshments? I can ask Mrs Hudson to prepare some sandwiches, perhaps?'

'Thank you, a cup of tea would be delightful, but nothing else.'

When Mrs Hudson had brought the tea, Holmes went on, 'I take it that it is this matter of Lord Hammerford's will that brings you here?'

'It is, Mr Holmes,' said Lady Lewis, her voice taut.

Holmes waited, and when Lady Lewis said nothing further, he ventured, 'It is in many ways an odd business, and perhaps a rather sad one.'

'You are correct as to that, Mr Holmes.' Lady Lewis hesitated again, and then her feelings evidently overcame her natural reticence. 'Oh,' she cried, 'I wish I had never heard of Lord Hammerford, or his stupid will! No,' she went on, as Holmes leaned forward in his chair, 'I am not going to burst into tears, or anything silly of that sort. But George has told me something of what has happened since we heard of the will, and I wish to Heaven that it were all over, for I can see nothing good coming of it all.'

Holmes said nothing, and Lady Lewis continued, 'As I say, George has told me something of what happened earlier today, Mr Holmes, and I came to apologize and to explain. In the ordinary course of events, you know, George would never do anything at all underhand — oh, he has been foolish at times, I know that better than anyone, but he is as honest as the day is long. But the thought of this great fortune has clouded his judgement somewhat. Why, he would not normally have dreamed of doing anything so unsporting as to hinder an opponent!'

'You refer to the fact that he destroyed one of the clues, I take it?' said Holmes.

Lady Lewis nodded. 'And then Doctor Watson so far forgetting his manners as to threaten him with a stick! Why, he likes Doctor Watson, and even went so far as to describe the doctor as "a delightful old chap" to me.'

' "Old", Lady Lewis?' I asked.

'Oh, that is just his way, Doctor,' she said quickly.

'Well, he struck me as a pleasant enough old fellow, too, I must say. As for threatening him, I am genuinely sorry for that, and I shall be grateful if you say as much to your husband when you see him. I do not think I would have gone so far as to strike him, but his behaviour was really most provoking.'

'And that is precisely why I have come to see you,' said Lady Lewis. 'I know that under ordinary circumstances you would none of you behave in this childish and belligerent manner. The thought of this fortune is making you all act like fools!'

'Well, that is frank enough in all conscience,' said Holmes, at something of a loss as to how best to reply.

Lady Lewis drew herself up in her chair. 'I am very sorry if I offend you, gentlemen, but that is how it seems to me. And I include my own husband in the catalogue, and have said as much to his face. As for this other dreadful business, I scarcely know what to make of it, strangers in the house to make sure we are safe, my husband followed everywhere, myself forbidden to go out unaccompanied — it is intolerable, Mr Holmes. Intolerable!'

'And what would you suggest?' asked Holmes, no whit perturbed.

Lady Lewis subsided, and thought in silence for a time. 'The only way out that I can see is for you all to work together somehow, find the treasure, and defeat these ruffians who threaten our happiness.'

Holmes sat back in his chair, a mixture of triumph and frustration upon his face. 'Believe me, madam, I have tried,' he told her. 'Watson here will agree that it was the first thing I suggested, but I am merely acting as an agent, and must obey the instructions of my principal.'

'But can you not convince Sir James, Mr Holmes?'

'If I could, can you convince Sir George, madam?'

'I flatter myself that I can.' There was a steely edge to Lady Lewis's voice which, for all the lady's beauty of form and face, boded no good for Sir George were he to remain unconvinced, I thought.

'I believe you could,' said Holmes. He leaned back in his chair and stared at the ceiling.

'More tea, Lady Lewis?' I asked, to fill the awkward pause.

'Yes, thank you, Doctor.'

I poured the tea, and Lady Lewis drank in silence, evidently unwilling to disturb Holmes, as it seemed to me. For my part, I could not see what he might suggest that would make things easier for all of us.

As so often, I underestimated him. At the end of some five minutes, he suddenly let out a little exclamation, and leaned forward again. 'Of course!' he said eagerly. 'Lady Lewis, what I propose is just this. Your husband, Sir George, I mean, will share with us the clue which he found and destroyed, as a token of his good faith. For my part, I will undertake to convince Sir James that it is imperative that we all work together against our common enemy. As for any division of the treasure, should we succeed in finding it, that will have to be by mutual discussion between Sir James and Sir George, although I shall put forth myself as a disinterested umpire. What do you say to that?'

'Excellent, Mr Holmes!' Lady Lewis fairly clapped her hands at this, while I regarded Holmes with what I hoped was a suitably sceptical gaze. Impervious he may be to the finer emotions, harshly does he speak of them, but they have served him well enough on many an occasion, and behold here was yet another instance. Naturally, he was careful to avoid my eye.

Lady Lewis was starting to get to her feet, and I stood up to assist her. 'You say Peterson is here?' I asked. 'Yes? Well, you should be safe enough, for he is a good fellow. Will you take a cab, though?' I added, with some hesitation, for I had a strong suspicion that she might not be able to afford the luxury, whilst at the same time I did not want her to think that I was hinting any such thing.

'Oh, yes. I have a little money of my own, and I keep tight hold of that. I find it the best way.' The hint of steel was back again. With such a woman at his side, I was somewhat astonished that Sir George had not been compelled to mend his ways; still, there was time, for they had not been married long, if I recollected aright.

Holmes and I escorted Lady Lewis to the street door, and I was just about to call for Billy and ask him to fetch Peterson from the kitchen when the door bell rang. As I was at the door it was pointless to stand on ceremony, so without waiting for Billy or the maid, I opened the door, to reveal Sir James standing on the step, with young Lord Hammerford at his side. The pretty little nursemaid stood close by Sir James's carriage, which brightened the day for me, although under the circumstances I was most pleased to note that the sturdy driver seemed on the alert, and that he had a great stick on the seat beside him. Evidently he was prepared to repel any assailant.

'The lad was bored,' Sir James explained, 'so I thought I'd bring him here, let him pester Mrs Hudson, if that's all right.' He caught sight of Lady Lewis, and added, 'But perhaps I am intruding? I had thought that perhaps your business was concluded, madam.'

'It is, Sir James,' Lady Lewis told him. 'I am just leaving.'

'In that case, my carriage is entirely at your disposal.'

'Thank you, it is most kind. I shall not refuse your very kind offer, and shall send it back at once, of course.' Lady Lewis made as if to leave, but as she passed young Lord Hammerford she paused. 'He has had a curious and troubled start in life, has he not?' she asked no-one in particular. 'And yet he is surely deserving of better things.' And suddenly, impulsively, she bent down and embraced the young aristocrat, who did not seem to mind in the least. The rest of us tried to look away as best we could.

'I am sorry,' said Lady Lewis, standing up after a few moments, 'but I could not resist it. Sir George and I have not been blessed with children of our own, but the maternal instinct is a powerful and wonderful one.'

'It is indeed,' murmured Holmes.

Lady Lewis went on, 'I wonder — it is such a fine afternoon, it seems a pity that the boy should be cooped up indoors, even with dear Mrs Hudson to look after him. May I not further avail myself of your kind offer of your carriage, Sir James, and take him for a drive? With your permission, of course, Mr Holmes. We might visit the Park.'

'I am not at all sure about the Park,' said Holmes quickly.

'Oh, but there is no danger, surely? You can easily see anyone who approaches, and I shall have Sir James's driver and Peterson to look after me.'

Holmes frowned. 'Sir James?'

'As I say, you may regard my carriage as your own,' said Sir James to Lady Lewis. He turned to Holmes. 'I suppose a drive of sorts would not be too dangerous, would it?'

'And a stroll in the Park?' asked Lady Lewis again.

Sir James looked again at Holmes, who shrugged, and said, 'I must insist that you do not move far from the carriage, though, and that Peterson goes with you. If you have the slightest suspicion,' he told Sir James's driver, 'return here at once, and do not stop for anyone.'

The driver nodded and touched his hat in a significant fashion with his stick, as if to indicate that he fully understood his duties. Peterson was duly summoned from the kitchen, the little party climbed into the carriage, and Peterson climbed up behind, looking, I must say, quite splendid in his uniform.

'Two stout fellows,' said Sir James, as we waved them off. 'They should be safe enough, don't you think?'

Holmes did not seem entirely convinced. 'I have half a mind to run after them and insist that they remain here,' said he. 'Or else that we should accompany them. I have grave doubts, Sir James.'

'Peterson is a good chap,' I told him. 'And I wouldn't care to meet that driver in a dark alley.'

'Perhaps you are right,' said Holmes, drumming upon the door with his fingers. He turned to go into the house, and I could have sworn that I heard him mutter, 'Damnation!' under his breath, but I cannot be certain. Aloud, he said, 'Since you are here, Sir James, we might as well have a council of war, and consider our next move.' And he led the way upstairs to our sitting room, and flung himself into an armchair.

'Brandy and soda, Sir James?' I asked. 'And a cigar?'

'Thank you, Doctor. Now, Mr Holmes, what have you in

mind?'

'Lady Lewis came here to communicate her distress at the turn which events have taken. Like me, she is strongly of the opinion that the best interests of all of us will be served by co-operation. I am bound to say that I entirely agree, and I reiterate my original suggestion of working together as much as may with Sir George.'

Sir James shook his head at once.

'I must ask you to reconsider,' said Holmes. 'Bear in mind that Sir George has a clue which we have not. We cannot keep him under observation indefinitely, so what would your course of action be?'

Sir James frowned, but said nothing.

Holmes went on, 'Would you really have Watson here beat the information out of him?'

'It wouldn't be the first time a delicate matter has been settled in an indelicate manner by a couple of roughs with bludgeons after dark,' muttered Sir James.

'And you really think that would do the trick?' asked Holmes sceptically. 'In any event, I rather fancy Sir George would give as good as he got. If we fail to secure the treasure for ourselves, then the best — the very best, Sir James — that we can hope for is that Sir George is some-how prevented from getting to it as well. Legally, you can do nothing, for the will is quite specific.'

'And what do you suggest, then?' asked Sir James.

'Lady Lewis has agreed to persuade her husband to share the clue with us.'

'In return for what, precisely? What terms?'

Holmes shrugged. 'That will be a matter for yourself and Sir George to discuss, when — or perhaps one should err on the side of caution and say "if" — we find the treasure.'

Sir James frowned. 'If, and I echo your caution and say that it is a very big "if", if I were to agree to this suggestion, then I think it might be better to agree terms at the outset.'

'As you wish. If you recall, I suggested that before ever we began this business.'

'I recall it, sir,' said Sir James with a frown. 'Well, and suppose I agree to this, what terms do you think I should suggest? What sort of division would seem equitable to you?'

'As a starting point, I suggest ten per cent to Sir George,' said Holmes. 'After all, he is only related by marriage to the previous Lord Hammerford, which gives the boy a somewhat better claim. Unless, that is, the grandfather's suspicions were justified,' he added thoughtfully.

'Oh, Mr Holmes, I thought we'd dismissed all that nonsense!' said Sir James with a touch of impatience.

'It may be that Sir George will bring the matter up on his side of the negotiations, use that as an argument for a bigger share for himself,' Holmes pointed out.

'H'mm. Even ten per cent would, of course, amount to fifty thousand pounds in hard cash. It is a hefty amount.'

'But there would remain four hundred and fifty thousand.'

'And the value of the gems and what have you may well have increased in the last couple of years,' I pointed out. 'That may well cover the amount we are thinking of.'

Sir James sat for a moment in thought. 'Would an initial offer of ten thousand seem parsimonious, do you think?'

'Niggardly,' remarked Holmes shortly.

'Penny-pinching, I should have said,' I told Sir James.

He laughed. 'You may be right, though my own feeling is that I owe it to the boy to secure the best division that I can.' He leaned forward and looked directly at Holmes. 'Very well, I agree to your overall suggestion, if not to your specific stipulations as to any division of the spoils. After all, you cannot expect me to throw away young Lord Hammerford's inheritance without a struggle, can you?'

'I am perfectly happy to leave the discussions as to exact terms to you,' said Holmes. 'All I want at this juncture is to secure your agreement to our co-operating with Sir George in order to recover the treasure.'

'In that case, sir, you have my word.'

'I am glad to hear it. Now, I think we should go round and see Sir George at once,' said Holmes. 'The sooner we can start working together, the safer we shall be.'

'Safer?' said Sir James. 'Oh, you are thinking of this gang of rogues, is that it?'

Holmes nodded. 'They are not bound by our gentlemen's agreement, you see. It is my opinion that Sir George is in very grave danger at this moment,' he said. 'The only consolation is that he is well attended by our irregulars, though he does not know it. Still, for all their sterling qualities they are only boys, and can do little against desperate men, other than report what has occurred, and the blow may fall at any time.'

In this, he was right, but only partially right, for it was not upon Sir George that the blow fell. We had gathered together hats and coats ready to leave, when there was a sharp ring at the street door, followed immediately by what I can only call a pounding, as of a very large fist, upon it. Holmes and I gazed at each other with a wild surmise, like the chaps on a hill in Darien. 'Hullo,' said Holmes, 'here's trouble, or I'm much mistaken!'

Our sitting room door flew open, and Billy charged in without knocking or other preliminaries. He evidently had news of some urgency to impart, but all he could manage was a sort of incoherent stammer. Holmes pushed him gently to one side, and flew down the stairs, with Sir James, Billy and myself at his heels.

A large policeman stood in the doorway. At his side stood the little nursemaid who had charge of young Lord Hammerford. Holmes muttered an imprecation, and asked, 'Well, constable?'

'Beg pardon, Mr Holmes, but there's been a spot of bother.'

The nursemaid, unable to keep silent, broke in, 'There was a gang of them, sir. John and that nice Mr Peterson, they tried to fight them off but there was too many of them. They've took her ladyship, and young Lord Hammerford!' And after saying this she burst, quite understandably, into tears.

SEVEN

Sir James swore heartily and imaginatively for a moment or so, and I fancy that the odd unparliamentary expression escaped my own lips. What with our own consternation so freely expressed, and the policeman trying to explain matters in his stolid fashion, and the nursemaid still in floods of tears, you will readily appreciate that there was a certain amount of confusion for a time.

Holmes at last held up a hand for silence. 'You see what comes of your shilly-shallying!' he told Sir James bitterly. 'Still, it is too late now for recriminations. All that we can do is attempt to salvage what we may from this unhappy situation. Tell me,' he asked the nursemaid, 'what exactly happened? You were in the Park, you say?'

The girl sniffled, and I handed her a handkerchief. 'Yes, sir,' she told Holmes, as she wiped her eyes. 'Her ladyship stopped the carriage, what with it being such a pleasant afternoon, and got out with Lord Hammerford. Mr Peterson, he got down too, to look after them, as it were, as you'd ordered him to, so none of us was expecting anything out of the way. Well, they hadn't gone no more than a few yards when a young couple with a baby in a carriage came up to them, and the young lady, she starts making a fuss of Lord Hammerford, you know how they do, sir? Anyway, before any of us had realized what was going on, the young man, he attacked Mr Peterson, and the young lady had grabbed her ladyship and Lord Hammerford and run off with them! Only it wasn't a young lady at all,' she added, with another loud sob, 'it was a man dressed up!'

'This abominable business of dressing up in women's clothes!' exclaimed Sir James. 'I'd horsewhip the blighters!'

'I have occasionally found such a disguise exceedingly useful myself,' murmured Holmes. 'Though I always assume it unwillingly and as a very last resort,' he added hastily, lest there should be any silly misunderstanding on this point. 'What was the coachman, John, is it, doing?' he asked the nursemaid.

'Well, sir, of course he jumped down off the seat and tried to help, but there was too many of them. More of them seemed to leap out from nowhere, to materialize, as you might say, from the bushes. It all happened so fast, you see.'

'H'mm, It was evidently carefully planned,' said Holmes. 'But Peterson and John are not with you now? Where are they?'

'The doctor's looking at them, sir.'

'There's a doctor's surgery not far from where it happened, sir,' added the constable. 'We called him at once.'

'I see. Are they badly hurt, do you know?'

'The doctor didn't seem to think so, sir,' said the constable. 'Cuts and bruises, but no worse than that. More a question of hurt pride, as it were, if you ask me.'

'I see.'

'You think this is the gang of which you spoke?' Sir James asked Holmes.

'Oh, I'm quite certain of that. It bears their stamp. The first attempt with a single man taking his chances having proved unsuccessful, they planned this one on a larger scale. Tell me,' Holmes asked the nursemaid, 'was one of these villains a big man, looked a bit like a professional boxer?'

'Beg pardon, sir, but there was a few of them looked like that.'

'H'mm. Well then, was one of them a little rat-like fellow?'

The nursemaid started at this. 'Yes, sir. Well, I'd have said more like a weasel.'

'The precise analogy is of no consequence,' said Holmes. 'This is undoubtedly the gang which has been following us, and Sir George.' He mused for a moment, then added, 'Well, perhaps that is fortunate.'

'Fortunate, Holmes?' I asked, incredulous.

'At any rate it narrows things down somewhat, does it not?' Holmes seemed to fall into a sort of reverie at this point, causing Sir James to give a theatrically exaggerated gasp of disbelief.

The constable, too, showed signs of restlessness. 'Beg pardon, Mr Holmes,' he said, 'but what should I do now, sir?'

'Do?'

'Can't just ignore it, Mr Holmes, now can I?'

'Have you said anything to anyone else?' asked Holmes. 'Are there more of your colleagues looking into the matter?'

'No, sir. I've hardly had time to let anyone know, as you might say. The doctor, of course, but no-one official, like. This young person insisted we bring you the news before doing anything else.'

'You did well. By rights, of course, you should report this to your superiors,' said Holmes thoughtfully. 'However, that would only mean a large number of officers getting in the — that is, getting involved. I really must think hard about the best course to take, if you will excuse me a moment,' and his face grew dreamy again.

Very often in my long association with Holmes have I been strongly tempted to assault him, for his habit of ignoring his associates completely for long periods can be most trying to the temper of even an extremely tolerant man such as myself. This was one such occasion. The policeman was shifting his weight from foot to foot, Sir James was mumbling oaths under his breath, and I myself was just about ready to seize Holmes by the collar and shake him into some sort of activity. However, so serene was his demeanour that none of us ventured to disturb him again for a long two minutes; and even then it was not one of us who disrupted his train of thought, but Sir George Lewis, who arrived in a cab, ran headlong up our steps, in at the door which stood ajar, and demanded, 'Have you heard what's happened?'

'What, then?' asked Holmes, the thread of his thoughts broken. 'Oh, you mean this abduction business?'

'Damn it all, man, can there be more than one such disaster in a single day?' asked Sir George with understandable vigour.

Holmes stared at him. 'Forgive me,' he said, 'I was so very much absorbed with trying to ascertain our best course of action that I had all but forgotten that there is a human element to the whole thing.' He shook himself, like one who wakes from a dream.

'Well?' Sir George inquired. 'What is your conclusion? Or have you not yet reached one? Do you perhaps need to stand day-dreaming here for a further couple of hours before proceeding?'

'Proceeding where, pray?' asked Holmes mildly.

'Why, to the Park, of course! Is that not where this outrage took place?'

'It is indeed,' said Holmes, his manner as placid as ever, 'but the kidnappers are hardly likely to be there still.' He waved a hand. 'The officer here, and this young lady, have just come from the Park, so there seems little point our returning there.'

Sir George subsided at once. 'You are right, of course, Mr Holmes,' he said. 'I must ask you to forgive me.'

'There is absolutely nothing to forgive,' said Holmes. 'You are very naturally concerned at what has taken place. But what, on calmer reflection, would you have us do?'

'Rescue them, of course!' exclaimed Sir George. He stopped, thought for a moment, then added, 'But when you put me on the spot, I confess I cannot imagine how we might best achieve that end. Will you not come to the Park, though,' he added in a more composed but still anxious voice, 'and let us see if there is any clue as to where they have been taken?'

I added my two-pennyworth to the argument. 'Yes, Holmes, anything is better than this inactivity. We ought to be able to find some indication as to where best to start looking. Or you ought, at any rate.'

'Oh, as to that,' said Holmes in an off-hand way, 'I fancy I could set my hand upon them within ten minutes.'

'What?' I think everyone in that hallway, Holmes alone

excepted, shouted the word at once.

'Yes, that was never the question. The question is just this: shall we be better leaving them there? I rather incline to the opinion that we shall.'

At that point, two things happened. I started to say, 'How do you know where they are?' or something of that sort; but I had not articulated more than the first word or two when Sir George rushed towards Holmes in a very significant fashion.

''Ere!' said the constable, interposing his bulky frame between Sir George and Holmes, who seemed unaware of any peril.

'You really should not joke about such things,' Sir George told Holmes, barely holding himself in check with an obvious effort.

Holmes stared at Sir George. 'You really must control your emotions,' he told him sternly. 'Watson here will tell you that although my sense of humour is at times a trifle distorted, I do not joke about matters as serious as this. When I say that I know where these villains are, I mean it quite literally.'

'But how can you possibly know that, Holmes?' I asked.

'I know that because, on the very first day of this most interesting case, I followed the man who had been sent to follow you, Sir George. You may recall that I absented myself for a short while in the afternoon, Watson?'

'I do. But in the name of Heaven, if you know where they are, then how can you hesitate for a single instant as to whether or not to attempt a rescue?'

'Ah, that is the old soldier speaking, the man of action. And Sir George here, another man of action, evidently concurs. But consider carefully,' said Holmes earnestly, 'that these rogues, reprobate though they are, did not intend any harm to come to Lady Lewis, or to young Lord Hammerford. Had they wished to hurt them, kill them even, they could have done that quite well in the Park, then and there, without going to all the trouble of spiriting them away. Do you agree? Good. No, the sole purpose of taking them is to use them as hostages, to parlay for an exchange, the money for the two precious lives. That being so, these kidnappers will be sure to keep them safe. Indeed, and I am quite well aware that this will not strike you at once as being sensible, but they will probably be safer there than anywhere else, for the blow has fallen, so to speak, and now we need not fear it falling. You comprehend? I strongly suspect that if we went through this door now, we should not be followed, for now they have no need to keep watch on us. They have us, they think, where they want us, and so have nothing to fear from us and no need to keep us under observation. We can now direct all our energies to a successful solution of the case without worrying about either being followed everywhere or the safety of our loved ones.' And he looked from one to another of us, as if seeking approval of this monstrous scheme.

Sir George was the first to speak. 'There is a certain specious logic in your argument, Mr Holmes,' he said, controlling himself with a perceptible effort of will, 'but frankly it seems to me that it is very much more specious than logical. As to these villains not harming my wife and the boy, you are doing nothing more than surmising there. My wife is somewhat highly-strung, and the thought of what she will endure cooped up in some rat-hole is more than I can bear!'

'And what of the boy?' I added. 'It can hardly have been pleasant for him to be snatched away in that brutal fashion, can it, Holmes? He will want his familiar surroundings, his nursery, his toys, his cosy little circle.'

'They are right, Mr Holmes,' said Sir James, by way of concluding the matter. 'As to this business of their being safe with these rogues, why, words fail me! If it's safety you want for them, return them to me and I'll personally guarantee a company of guardsmen. A regiment, two, if you specify it. You know I can undertake to do that,' he added significantly.

'Very well,' said Holmes. 'I see I am out-voted. The question now becomes: how? The direct method, the large-scale frontal attack which has, I am sure, occurred immediately to each and every one of you, has its potential dangers. If any harm were — God forbid! — to come to the prisoners, it would be most likely to come about in the confusion of such an attack, and the short tempers that would naturally be engendered. No, we need a plan. We need subtlety. We need a diversion. We need —' The ringing of the door bell cut short his list of requirements.

We had still not moved from the hallway, and as I was nearest the door and had already been acting as a sort of temporary unofficial butler, I opened the door, reflecting to myself that although the matter was momentous enough in all conscience, yet this constant stream of visitors none the less had something of the quality of a stage farce about it.

That impression was reinforced by the young man who stood nervously upon the step, for he looked for all the world like a second-rate actor from a third-rate touring company. He was perhaps twenty-five years of age, with curly and rather untidy brown hair under a bowler hat, which he removed and twisted in his hands as I pulled the door open. He wore a long coat which had once been fashionable but was now showing signs of wear and tear, and round his neck was a broad leather strap upon which hung a leather satchel or dispatch case of some sort.

'Well?'

'Ah, yes,' said he, gazing at the little knot of folk inside the hallway with a certain amount of bemusement. 'Forgive me, sir. It was Sir George Lewis I was looking for. I fancy I saw him come in here?'

Sir George stepped forward from the shadows. 'I am he,' he said. 'But I do not think I have the honour of your acquaintance?'

'No. That is, my name is Wainwright, Douglas Wainwright. I fear I have no card with me —'

Sir George waved aside the social niceties. 'What is it you want, Mr Wainwright? I am a trifle preoccupied just at the moment, so I beg you to be as brief as humanly possible, sir.'

'It was by way of being a rather personal matter, Sir George,' said Mr Wainwright hesitantly.

'Oh, no secrets here, man. You may speak before these gentlemen — and ladies,' added Sir George, waving a hand to include the little nursemaid, and Mrs Hudson, who had emerged unbidden and unseen from her kitchen to investigate, 'exactly as you would before me'.

Mr Wainwright cleared his throat delicately, and began to unfasten the straps on his satchel. 'As you wish, Sir George,' said he, 'although I would have preferred it otherwise. I have here, sir, your notes of hand, to a grand total of three hundred and seventy-two pounds, six shillings and —' And that was as far as he got.

I have tried to indicate in this account that Sir George Lewis, though a stout chap, a fine fellow, and all the other platitudinous expressions indicative of approbation, was none the less a man of action, a man of pronounced forcefulness of opinion. Not, in short, a man to suffer fools at all, much less gladly.

A curious look had started to come upon Sir George's face as Mr Wainwright began speaking, and I could read it as easily as I read my own notes; easier, indeed, these days, as my handwriting has latterly taken on some crab-like characteristics. Sir George may have been thwarted in his legitimate desire to wreak vengeance upon Holmes by that officious ass of a policeman, that look said to me, but he was damned if he would be thwarted by anyone in his desire to wreak vengeance upon this wretched creature who intruded at this critical juncture in Sir George's life to dun him for three hundred and seventy-two pounds, six shillings and however many pence it might have been.

In short, at the point which I have indicated in the unfortunate Mr Wainwright's speech, Sir George sprang upon him like the proverbial tiger. I had, as I say, half expected something of the sort, and I lost no time in grabbing hold of Sir George's collar and attempting to drag him away. Holmes and the police constable joined in, and between us we separated Sir George from his prey, and picked up Mr Wainwright, who had lost his footing and crashed to the linoleum.

'Really, Sir George!' said Mr Wainwright, when he had

recovered his breath, adding, 'Hardly expected this from a gentleman,' and, 'Purely a matter of business,' and similar phrases as he dusted himself down ostentatiously.

'If we have all quite finished?' said Holmes. 'Perhaps we would all be more comfortable in our sitting room, where we can discuss this matter more quietly. Mrs Hudson, perhaps you would take this young lady and give her some tea?' he added, indicating the nursemaid. And without waiting for an answer he led the way upstairs.

I looked at Mrs Hudson and shrugged my shoulders, by way of an apology for Holmes's brusqueness, but she knew his ways as well I do myself and merely gave a taut little smile. I turned and followed the others upstairs.

EIGHT

'Now, Mr Douglas Wainwright,' said Holmes in a steely voice, 'perhaps you would sit down and tell us your story? We are, I know, all eager — nay, positively agog — to hear it.'

Mr Wainwright looked round the sitting room, which seemed full to overcrowding. His gaze took in Holmes, Sir George, Sir James, the policeman, whose name I had gathered was Perkins, and lastly myself. And I fancy he did not see one particularly friendly face amongst the entire collection. 'Er — perhaps I'll stand,' ventured Mr Wainwright, but Holmes guided him gently but firmly to a chair.

'Your tale?' prompted Holmes again. 'And I may add that, as you will perhaps have guessed, we are in no mood for prevarication or procrastination.'

'In other words, the truth — and quick!' Sir George expounded, tapping his stick against the palm of his left hand in a sinister fashion.

Mr Wainwright swallowed hard. 'It is purely a matter of business,' he protested feebly. 'Constable,' he appealed to Perkins, 'I call upon you to witness that I have been attacked entirely without —'

'None of your lip, my lad,' said Perkins shortly. 'You just answer Mr Holmes, and be quick about it.'

'Well, then, but I do so under protest. I have a regular job, which brings me a reasonable income,' Wainwright began. 'A month or so back, I received a small inheritance, a touch under thirty pounds, from an unexpected source. Now, in the ordinary course of events I would have deposited it in the savings bank, but I was feeling a bit reckless. I happened to overhear a conversation in a public house, two chaps discussing the stock market, and one of them was singing the praises of a mining stock. I asked at a firm of brokers, and they seemed to think it was hopeless, but they made no difficulty about acting for me and buying a few shares. Well, the price doubled within a week, and I sold the shares before anything could go wrong.

'A pal of mine, to whom I told the story, said my luck was in, and gave me a hot tip for a horse race. By all the laws of moral rectitude, I should have lost the lot, but I didn't. The horse romped home at eight to one, and I found myself with four hundred pounds to play with. Now, I could have played safe, put it in the bank, even considered buying a small business. But once again I had a fancy to speculate, see if I could run it up a little more. I happened to see a note of the late Lord Hammerford's will in the paper, and I got into conversation with the same pal who'd given me the tip on the horse. He's a real character, knows everything that's going on, or at any rate he appears to, and he told me that there was something odd about the will. Well, I went along to Somerset House and paid my half-crown to see the will. I couldn't see that it took me very far, but when I mentioned the details to this pal of mine, he whistled when I mentioned the name of Sir George Lewis. Forgive me, Sir George,' he added with an anxious look at that gentleman, 'but he evidently knew you by reputation, and he mentioned something of your financial difficulties.'

'And, in short, you decided to buy up Sir George's debts?' concluded Holmes.

Wainwright nodded. 'It seemed a safe investment, considering Sir George's circumstances. And as I am myself involved, as you might say, in the world of finance, it seemed safer than betting on horses and what have you.'

'H'mm. And you say you did this entirely on your own initiative?' asked Holmes.

'Why, yes.'

'No-one else involved at all, even this mysterious "pal" of yours?'

'No, Mr Holmes. It was just a conversation, a talk in the saloon bar. Of course I bought him a few drinks and a box of cigars when the horse won, and I'd have done the same again if I'd made anything out of this other scheme. But why do you ask?'

'Would it interest you to know that you are not the only man to have been tempted by the terms of the will to grasp a share of this great wealth?'

'Oh? I assure you, I bought the paper in all good faith. If there are others dunning Sir George, then —'

'These others use methods which are more direct and much less civilized than your own,' said Holmes. 'To put it plainly, sir, these villains have kidnapped Lady Lewis and young Lord Hammerford, and they undoubtedly plan to attempt to use them to extort the inheritance from its rightful owners.'

'Good Lord!' Wainwright's face turned white at this. 'I can only repeat, Mr Holmes, that I have nothing to do with anything like that, or with anyone else who may be involved in this matter.' He scrabbled with the strap of his case again. 'In fact, I shall tear up this paper now, while you all watch! And that way, you will be sure that I have nothing to gain from this dreadful crime.'

Sir George held up a hand. 'No need for that, Mr Wainwright,' he said. 'Business is business, as I think you remarked just now. I have every intention of redeeming my notes at the earliest opportunity, so you hang on to them. But you see now why I was less than polite when you first rang the door bell?'

'Indeed, yes. Doubtless you thought I was one of these villains, or something of the kind?' And poor Mr Wainwright shivered at the thought of it.

'Well, Mr 'Olmes,' said Perkins rather ponderously, 'that's sorted that little puzzle out very nicely, as you might say, but I don't see as how it takes us much further with the other, more pressing, matter.'

'Quite right,' agreed Sir James.

'Oh, I don't know,' said Holmes. He was about to elaborate when the bell of the street door rang. 'I wonder who that is?' he asked of the room in general.

'Well, at least I don't have to answer it this time!' I muttered to myself.

A moment later Billy tapped at the door, and announced that Sir James's driver and Peterson had returned, not very much the worse for their experiences. 'Send them up, Billy,' said Holmes, and in a very short time they had entered the room, looking rather sheepish. Peterson had a great bandage round his head, having, it turned out, been struck with a club of some sort; and John, the coachman, had a few cuts and bruises. But they both insisted that they were in first-class condition, and desired to be included in any plan which Holmes might formulate.

'And have you formulated any plan, Mr Holmes?' asked Sir James.

'I venture to think so.' Holmes asked Wainwright, 'You say you are yourself employed in the world of finance?'

'In a very small way, Mr Holmes.'

'And may I ask what that way might be?'

'Well.' Wainwright coughed, then tapped his satchel. 'The fact is, I'm a rent-collector.'

'I rather deduced as much,' said Holmes.

'Oh, it isn't a very exciting job, I know, but it's honest. And, as I said, it brings me in an acceptable wage each week.'

'I am sure it does,' said Holmes. 'Tell me, have you a rent book with you at the moment?'

Wainwright frowned. 'For which properties in particular, Mr Holmes?'

'Why, that scarcely matters. For any. Have you a rent book of some sort there?'

Wainwright nodded, and produced a thick leather-bound book from his case. 'Will that do?' he asked, as puzzled as the rest of us.

'It will do capitally,' said Holmes. 'Now, are you willing to help us to recover Lady Lewis and young Lord Hammerford?'

'Of course,' said Wainwright at once. 'I am at your disposal.'

'Very well,' said Holmes. 'You see, most of us are known to these villains, but you, Mr Wainwright, are not, and that circumstance is likely to prove exceedingly useful.'

And he went on to outline his plan.

Five minutes later, we were in the street. 'We can use Sir James's carriage,' said Holmes, 'and I think another cab will suffice. Billy?' Billy whistled loudly, and a cab pulled across the road. 'Now, gentlemen,' said Holmes, 'if we are all quite ready? Not you, Billy,' he added, as the pageboy prepared to climb into the cab he had summoned. 'I cannot expose you to possible danger.'

Billy looked positively downcast at this. 'Please, Mr 'Olmes? Just this once?'

I added my voice to that of the pageboy. 'Why not, Holmes? He could stay in the background, ready to carry messages and what have you. Might be useful. As for any danger, I think your scheme is pretty well foolproof there. Billy will be in no greater danger than the rest of us.'

'Very well. But you must stay well out of the way.'

Billy, delighted, leapt into the cab, and the rest of us either followed him or got into Sir James's carriage.

'You're quite sure you have the right place, Holmes?' I asked anxiously as we rattled along.

'I am certain.'

'But it might be nothing more than the lodging of the one man you followed,' I pointed out.

Holmes shook his head. 'I stayed there long enough to ensure that several of the rascals came and went. I am satisfied that it is the place. Indeed, I fancy that I could hazard a guess at the very room where the hostages are being held, for I noticed bars at one window.' He tapped with his stick to tell the coachman to stop. 'We had best not get too close,' he told us. 'We can approach on foot from here.'

I got out of the carriage and looked around me. I did not recognize my surroundings, but it was certainly no very salubrious neighbourhood to which Holmes had brought us. I fancy that the City, the great commercial and financial heart of London, was not too far away in one direction, and the East End not too far in the other, but these squalid streets seemed to have nothing in common with any human locality that I had met with. I shivered, and moved closer to the others for companionship.

Holmes looked at Wainwright. 'You know the address? And what to do?'

'You may rely upon me implicitly, Mr Holmes.'

We had decided that the cab driver should remain behind, the promise of a double fee having secured his allegiance. And Peterson, who had taken something of a turn for the worse on the journey, was also left behind in Sir James's carriage, partly to watch that no harm came to it, and partly to act in some sort as a reserve force if needed. Holmes also suggested that Billy remain behind, but the pageboy rather demurred at this, and Holmes wasted no time on argument but agreed to let him go with us.

We went in a party as far as the corner, where Wainwright left us to approach the front door of the house which Holmes had indicated. The rest of us took a more circuitous route, through sordid back yards and alleyways, until we came into a narrow, foul-smelling lane. Holmes moved quietly along until we reached a broken-down gate, where he stopped, and motioned to us to be careful.

I moved to his side, and peeped over the gate, to see a common enough back yard, with the usual outbuildings of humble city housing. The place looked untidy, as if it had not been swept for ages. The house too looked run-down, the back door unpainted, and none too solid, to my eye. So much the better for Holmes's little scheme, I thought grimly.

The windows were grimy. Those on the upper storey were securely shut, and I could make out the one with bars which Holmes had mentioned. Grubby, faded curtains were drawn closed over that window, and I shuddered to think of the conditions under which Lady Lewis and the lad must be held.

The ground-floor windows, though, stood open. I have said that it was an ordinary back yard, and that means that it was not very large; barely spacious enough to contain those simple brick offices which I mentioned. And the house itself was an ordinary working-class abode, with perhaps two rooms on the ground floor. We could therefore hear sounds from inside the house without too much difficulty, and I caught some fragments of conversation, although I could not discern exactly what was being discussed. It sounded like some fairly convivial gathering, for there was the occasional burst of coarse laughter. I had no doubt that the rogues were thrashing out the division of the prospective spoils, or perhaps speculating as to how each would spend his own share.

At my side, Holmes glanced at his watch. 'Wainwright should be there now,' he whispered to me.

Almost as soon as he had said the words, there came a thunderous knocking at the front door of the house. The conversation from within ceased abruptly. The villains, I thought, had evidently not expected visitors.

Holmes dug an elbow in my ribs as Wainwright knocked again, louder this time. 'They dare not ignore him indefinitely,' he whispered in my ear, 'for he will knock until they answer, and the neighbours will eventually turn out to see what is amiss.' And he gave that low chuckle that had boded ill for so many criminals in the past.

Wainwright knocked yet again, and this time the door was thrown open with some vigour. Holmes motioned to me to advance into the yard, a safe enough process now, since the members of the gang would be concentrating their attention upon the events at the front door. I made my way cautiously inside the gate, then managed to move carefully right up to the back door. The others followed, finding what cover they might in the yard.

'It's the rent.' I heard Wainwright's rather plaintive voice at the front of the house.

'The rent?' A less refined voice altogether, that one, and with a note of aggression in it. 'What about the blinkin' rent, then?'

'It hasn't been paid,' said Wainwright. 'It's overdue, by some three months, and I need something on account, or the landlord will have to evict you. I have the books here, and everything.'

'Stay here, Billy,' said Holmes calmly over his shoulder. He looked at me, and I nodded.

'Something on account? Clear off, you so-and-so, or I'll give you something on account right enough!'

'It's no use blaming me,' said Wainwright, more plaintive than ever, 'I'm only doing my job, aren't I? Any violence and it's a police matter.'

'Police?' There was a worried note in the word, then the speaker raised his voice, shouting back into the house. ''Ere, Sammy, you pay the rent, don't yer? Come and deal with this silly beggar, will you?'

'Now, Watson,' said Holmes, and I put my shoulder to the flimsy door.

We burst into the place in a tight knot, and fairly charged through the couple of filthy rooms which comprised the accommodation. The little group of men by the front door turned in some surprise as we stormed in. Some evidently thought it was a police raid — possibly the earlier mention of the police had unsettled them, or it may have been the sight of PC Perkins in his uniform — and made their escape via the front door, Wainwright very sensibly standing aside to let them pass.

Some were more bold, and turned to fight. I judge that there were three or four of these more valiant companions, so we were pretty evenly matched. We had the advantage of surprise, and a slight superiority of numbers, although Holmes and Sir George both left us and ran upstairs after seeing that there was no real danger down here.

We were, of course, more concerned with freeing the captives than exacting vengeance, or capturing the criminals, and so we did not pursue them too far when they ran off, as they all did before very long.

We were taking a breather, and venturing to congratulate one another, when there was a terrific commotion at the head of the shabby staircase, and we looked round to see a large rough man — the same, I fancy, as we had encountered earlier — come charging down the stairs, taking them two or three at a stride. In itself, that would not have occasioned us too much heart-searching, but we were horrified to see that he held young Lord Hammerford clutched in his hefty arms.

For a moment, we stood there as if frozen, barely able to

comprehend what was happening. Then Perkins and I moved towards the foot of the stairs, just as the large man came crashing down the last few steps. His sheer bulk and momentum prevented our doing anything useful to stop him. Although Perkins was a big man, and I myself am no milksop, we were simply swept aside by the fellow as he crashed through us, and before we had properly recovered our poise, he had gone through the still open back door.

It seemed superfluous to tell one another to go after him. Such words as we did utter as we charged through the little house are hardly to be set down here. We shot out into the backyard, and came to an abrupt halt at the sight of Billy, grinning from ear to ear, and holding young Lord Hammerford in his arms. The large man was sprawled full length in the yard but before we could reach him he had scrambled up and taken to his heels.

'Trip him, did you, Billy?' I asked the pageboy.

He nodded. 'Went a right purler, 'e did,' he said appreciatively.

'Well done! I am only sorry I did not see it. Is the lad harmed at all?'

'Not 'im,' said Billy stoutly. 'Proper little 'ero, 'e is, and all.' This was true. In so far as his recent adventure had affected young Lord Hammerford, it seemed to have made him ready for further excitement; he appeared indeed to consider the whole affair as having been some sort of game, and it took the best efforts of Lady Lewis, who was also unharmed in any way, to calm him down. That done, he promptly went off to sleep.

'Now,' said Holmes, rubbing his hands, 'let's see what's come to our feast,' and he led the way back to the front door.

Our sole captive was the little shrimp of a man who had followed us at one point. He was clearly no hardened villain, and for a while I thought that he might need my professional services, for he seemed ready to faint at the thought of what lay in store. I was for letting him go, but PC Perkins said majestically that Justice must be done, and took the poor little fellow off.

'Well, Holmes,' I said, 'all's well that ends well.'

'Strikingly original, Watson,' he said with a laugh. 'But true enough, though. This chapter of our adventures has been concluded in a satisfactory fashion, but there remains the outstanding matter of the treasure. It seems somewhat churlish to bother Sir George just now,' he added, looking tolerantly at that gentleman, who was busily engaged upon comforting his wife in the traditional fashion, 'but tomorrow we must continue our search.'

NINE

'Well, Sir George?' asked Holmes.

It was the morning after the adventure which I have just recounted for you, and we were all four, Sir George, Sir James, Holmes and myself, sitting in our rooms at Baker Street.

Sir James had taken charge of Lady Lewis and young Lord Hammerford, who were now, according to Sir James, safer than the Bank of England and indeed as safe as Her Majesty herself. He would add nothing to this cryptic utterance, and bluntly refused to answer any of the questions I very naturally put to him; but his demeanour inspired every confidence.

'Sir George?'

Sir George yawned, excused himself, and said, 'I don't believe I thanked you gentlemen properly yesterday evening? I had other things on my mind,' and he flushed, and laughed awkwardly.

'No need for thanks, Sir George,' said Holmes. 'But I had actually intended more in the way of a delicate hint as to the clue which you discovered.'

'Oh, of course!' Sir George seemed nonplussed for a moment, then he went on, 'You are right, Mr Holmes. The clue, to be sure. Well, you saved my wife, and so I suppose you have certainly earned the right to know what it was.' He scribbled on a piece of paper, and handed it to Holmes, who glanced at it and passed it to me.

I read: 'Less than a palace, more than a house,' and on the next line, the cipher, 'R3/49.'

I looked at Sir George. 'The two phrases, if that is the right word, were on separate lines?'

He nodded. 'The whole thing was just as I have written it there.'

'Odd,' I mused. 'What can be less than a palace, more than a house? I suppose it must —'

'Hang on!' It was Sir George who interrupted me, and he clapped his hands over his ears as he did so.

I stared at him in some astonishment, and he uncovered his ears and said, 'You might at least let me leave the room before you begin your deliberations, Doctor.'

'But I thought we were working together now?' I asked, as bewildered as ever.

'Devil a bit of it,' said Sir George stoutly. 'What on earth could have given you that idea? We'd agreed to go our separate ways, had we not?'

Holmes, seemingly as confused as I was myself, looked at Sir George. 'But Lady Lewis assured me that we should be working together to solve the puzzle.'

'Did she, though? She never mentioned anything of the kind to me.'

Holmes frowned, then his face cleared. 'Ah, I see what has happened. Lady Lewis did indeed leave here yesterday promising to speak to you on the matter, but then the kidnapping took place and that, I suppose, caused the matter to slip her mind.'

'I expect you're right,' Sir George agreed cheerfully. 'Certainly I can tell you that whatever we may have spoken about last night, it wasn't this damned treasure hunt!' and his tanned face flushed again with embarrassment, but not entirely unmixed with pardonable pride and some pleasurable memories, as it seemed to me.

'This puts things in a rather different light,' said Holmes slowly. 'We had agreed with Lady Lewis that it would be much safer to work together, and to decide upon some reasonable apportionment of the fortune, either before we began our search together, or later when it should be safe in our hands.'

'A very sensible suggestion,' said Sir George. 'Still, as I say, my wife never broached the subject to me, and I think you will agree that a promise made on my behalf without actually consulting me first, even if it were made by my dear lady wife, can hardly be regarded as binding on me.'

Sir James threw his head back, and demanded loudly of the ceiling, 'What can be done with this fellow? He's quite impossible.'

Sir George laughed. 'As to that, Sir James, it was you, as I seem to recall, who rejected the notion of our working together right at the very outset.'

'True, but that was before I had properly realized the danger that we were in.'

'Oh, that can hardly matter now, can it?' asked Sir George. He appealed to Holmes, 'We have surely wrecked this gang's plans, have we not? There can be no possible question of our being in further danger, can there?'

Holmes shook his head. 'I fear you take too sanguine a view, Sir George. Oh, I cannot deny that we have spoiled one of their little schemes, but you may be certain they will lose no time in hatching another.'

'But what of the man we arrested last night?' I asked. 'I understood that Inspector Lestrade is questioning him at the moment.'

'True enough,' said Holmes, 'but even if Lestrade extracts the name of every member of the gang, and that is by no means guaranteed, they must still be traced and taken. And they will scarcely wait for the police to arrive. By now they will be in their lairs, safely hidden.'

'And so out of the way,' I said triumphantly.

'Not a bit of it,' said Holmes, shaking his head. 'They can emerge at any time, suitably disguised, can they not? And then, even if those particular villains did happen to be out of the running entirely, the gang's leaders will simply find new hirelings, unintelligent but obedient, to carry out their orders. For I can tell you with every assurance that the real villains, the genuine organizers of the whole scheme, were nowhere near that house last night. Indeed, by removing those villains whom we might recognize, we may well have made matters more difficult for ourselves, rather than less so, for the new troops will be unknown to us. A point which I seem to recollect attempting, unsuccessfully, to make yesterday,' he added with a frown.

'Ah, but the situation is still changed,' said Sir George. 'Now that the ones we hold dear are quite safe — and I am grateful beyond words for that, I can tell you, no argument there — then the only danger would be to ourselves. And which of us is so cowardly as to fear that?' he asked scornfully, looking round at us. 'Why, Mr Holmes, what could they do? If they kill me, it would simply mean they have lost a possible guide to the treasure. If they were to kidnap me, I hardly think that Sir James here would be willing to part with the cash to ransom me. And I'd feel much the same about him!'

It was Sir James's turn to laugh. 'There's a great deal of truth in what he says, Mr Holmes. Yes, let us each pursue our own line, and see what happens.'

'Will you not reconsider?' asked Holmes earnestly. 'Yesterday you were quite convinced, Sir James, and I am sure that you, Sir George, would have been persuaded. Had I insisted that we reach some agreement before I consented to reveal the hiding place, would you have stood out?'

'Perhaps not,' muttered Sir George. 'Under that sort of duress, with my wife's liberty and perhaps her very life at stake, I'd have agreed to anything. But the position has changed dramatically. Thanks entirely to you, I allow, Mr Holmes, but it has changed never the less, and I must act accordingly.'

'I entirely agree with Sir George,' said Sir James.

Holmes threw up his hands in despair. 'Very well, if you insist. But the responsibility for whatever happens is upon your shoulders, gentlemen.'

Sir George stood up. 'We may be on opposite sides temporarily,' he told us rather awkwardly, 'but for all that I'm truly grateful for your work last night. If anything had happened to my wife —'

Holmes raised a hand. 'As to that,' said he, 'I seem to recall that you were of considerable assistance in releasing young Lord Hammerford, so I think honours are pretty even there.'

Sir George smiled. 'Thank you, Mr Holmes. Well then,

we start from scratch, as it were. It's a pleasure to be matched with such honourable opponents, gentlemen, and there can be no disgrace involved in coming second. A thought which should console you somewhat.' And he shook hands with us all, and left us.

'Now, Watson,' said Holmes when the door had closed behind Sir George, 'the next clue.'

'Less than a palace, more than a house. A country estate? Oh, no, it is here in London that we must look. Unless, that is, old Lord Hammerford is directing us to his own estate in the north?'

Holmes shook his head. 'I hardly think so. The clues thus far have all been fairly local, so I cannot think that a dramatic change of scene is indicated at this stage. Still, it is a possibility, and we shall not reject it out of hand. Continue, Watson.'

'An hotel? That's more like it, these curious numbers might be "R" for a room number? Third floor, room forty-nine?'

'Well done, Watson, that is indeed more like it. But then would a man with a house in London need to stay at an hotel, I wonder? Another possibility, but I cannot think it is a probability. Something that is not quite a palace. Perhaps "house" in the business sense is meant? An office building? Palace, house, flat, lodgings, mansion —'

'Mansion House!' cried Sir James and I together.

Holmes leaned back and laughed aloud. 'Well done! Mansion House, of course.'

'And the numbers?' I asked.

'They mean as little to me as to you, Doctor. We shall just have to ask when we get there.' And Holmes stood up and sought his coat and hat.

We climbed into Sir James's carriage, and I was pleased to see that the coachman looked none the worse for yesterday's adventures, save that he sported a spectacular black eye. We were very soon bowling along, and as we turned into Oxford Street, heading towards Holborn, I could not forbear to say, 'A pity we didn't have this clue the other day, when we were walking up and down hereabouts. Might have saved us some time. And shoe leather.' Holmes did not bother to reply.

When we reached Mansion House, Holmes sought out the hall porter, who touched his cap civilly enough, but said, 'Beg pardon, gents, but the court's not open to visitors until twelve.'

'It was not that we were wanting,' said Holmes with a touch of impatience, and he mentioned the name of Lord Hammerford.

'Ah, yes, sir.' The porter's face cleared. 'If anyone was to name that gentleman,' he went on, reciting the next passage as if he had learned it by heart for such an occasion, 'I was to say that the cases in the middle of gallery number two at Guildhall would repay your attention.'

'And these numbers?' Holmes showed him the figures on a piece of paper.

The man shook his head. 'Don't mean a thing, sir. I'm sorry. Perhaps you'd best ask the porter or someone at the Guildhall, sir?'

'You are right,' said Holmes, handing the man a half-sovereign. 'Gentlemen?'

We returned to Sir James's carriage, and were very soon stopping outside the Guildhall. As everyone knows, it is open to visitors at all reasonable hours, and we lost no time in hurrying to gallery two. The case in the centre of the room holds a display of miniature paintings, and we examined these scrupulously, but search as we might there was nothing to be made of any of them.

'The porter at Mansion House was definite enough,' muttered Holmes.

'True — oh, but we have forgotten those odd numbers,' I told him.

'Ah, yes.' Holmes sought out an attendant, and showed him the scrap of paper, mentioning Lord Hammerford's name once again.

The man frowned. 'Question about the pictures, is it, sir? Best thing is to ask the keeper, sir. This way.'

We followed him along a corridor. He halted, tapped at a door and ushered us in. The room's occupant, a middle-aged man in a dark suit, rose as we entered. 'Yes?' he asked our guide.

'Beg pardon, sir, but these gentlemen were asking about a — Lord Hammerford, was it, sir?'

'That is correct,' said Holmes.

'I see. Thank you, Fletcher.' Our guide bowed, and left. The keeper waved us to seats.

Holmes introduced us, and the keeper said, 'Your names are familiar, gentlemen. What can I tell you about Lord Hammerford?'

'You knew him, then?' asked Holmes.

'Oh, yes. He was not what I might call a regular visitor, but I had the honour of some slight acquaintance with him.'

Holmes leaned forward and placed the piece of paper on

the keeper's desk. 'Does that mean anything at all to you, sir? I think it may relate to one of the miniatures in the gallery.'

'Why, yes. There is no mystery here, Mr Holmes. In common with most galleries these days, we have more pictures than we have space to exhibit, so a proportion is kept safely out of the way of the general public. What you have there is merely what we here would call a "reserve" number, hence the "R", and refers to one of those paintings not currently on display.'

'Ah. Could you tell us which painting is meant?'

'I can have it brought here,' said the keeper, ringing the bell on his desk. When an attendant arrived, the keeper gave him the slip of paper, with the request that the picture be brought to us. 'May I offer you a cigarette whilst we are waiting?' asked the keeper, and we accepted his kind offer, and made some desultory conversation.

In a short space of time the attendant returned, carrying one of the smallest paintings which I have ever seen, a true miniature, merely two inches by one and a half in size. The keeper produced a magnifying glass, but Holmes had already taken his lens from his pocket. Looking over his shoulder, I saw what to me seemed a fairly indifferent portrait of a gentleman in the costume of the fourteenth century. He sat at a table, a couple of keys in his hand, whilst through the window behind him was some sort of turret or tower.

'What do you know of this picture?' asked Holmes.

'The records are all here.' The keeper took a ledger from the shelf behind him, and glanced through it. 'Here we are. Remarkably little information, I fear. "Artist unknown, eighteenth century", I see.'

'H'mm. And the sitter?'

'Ah, that is easier. It is Mortimer, who had, you recall, formed an illicit liaison with Isabella, wife of the second Edward, and who was eventually executed by the third monarch of that name. The keys, I suppose, are to symbolize the keys of the kingdom, for Mortimer and Isabella effectively ruled for a scant couple of years, did they not, if memory serves me correctly?'

'Mortimer!' said Holmes.

'And one might say that Mortimer holds the key,' said I, laughing.

'Well done, Doctor!' But it was not Holmes who spoke. It was the mocking voice of Sir George, and I whirled round to see him standing in the open doorway, with the same attendant who had brought us here at his side.

'Beg pardon, sir —' the attendant began, but Sir George interrupted him.

'No need to trouble yourself further, my good man,' he said. 'I've learned what I came here to learn.' He gave us an ironic salute, and sped off back down the corridor.

'Damnation!' said Sir James. He stood up. 'Your pardon, sir,' he told the keeper, 'but I fear we really must be off as well. Our most sincere thanks to you, sir.'

'But —' But we were already crowding out into the corridor in pursuit of Sir George.

TEN

'Mortimer all along, eh?' I ventured as we rattled along in Sir James's carriage in hot pursuit of Sir George's cab. 'When I come to think about it, that explains why the sheets of paper were folded twice; to indicate that Mortimer held two secrets, not just the one.'

'Why the devil didn't the fellow say as much at the outset, then?' demanded Sir James with some warmth. 'I'll have something to say to Mortimer, and to the secretary too, about this, mark my words!'

'Ah, but then it was part of the game that he should not say too much,' Holmes pointed out. 'Had he done so the adventure would have been over before it had properly started and we should have missed many interesting events.'

'And,' I added, 'in point of strict, accurate fact, nobody ever asked Mortimer if he had the treasure in his keeping. I have my notebook here, and I see that Sir George asked if there might be a third set of envelopes, but that was all. None of us even thought of that! Although I see that I also put down "gnd lk CC" when I mentioned Mortimer in my notes.'

Sir James raised an eyebrow.

'"Grinned like a Cheshire Cat",' I explained.

'Ah. Well, I'll give the wretch something to grin for when I see him!'

'Sir James, you really must control your temper,' said Holmes severely. 'I cannot work with amateurs. And speaking of amateurs, Watson, fancy your bawling the solution out at the top of your voice like that, with Sir George standing at your very shoulder!'

'I could hardly be expected to know that the fellow was lurking in the wings, could I, Holmes? As to that, once you had mentioned the name "Mortimer" yourself, I imagine that Sir George could work out the answer readily enough!'

Holmes laughed. 'We are both to blame then. But there will be time enough later for recriminations,' he said. 'I can say honestly that I had thought the same as Sir George, that there might be yet another lot of envelopes,' he went on, 'but I must also confess it did not occur to me that there might be anything more valuable left in Mortimer's keeping. I was judging him on appearances, believing him merely a minor character in our little drama, and that is always unwise.'

'This does rather point up what I was saying earlier, though, Holmes,' I said. 'Old Mortimer — fine, sturdy chap, and all that — but he must be about a hundred years old! Suppose something had happened to him? What would have become of the clue then?'

'It is an interesting point,' Holmes admitted. 'But then it would be a monstrous coincidence were Mortimer to die, let us say, just after old Lord Hammerford had died, would it not?'

'But the portrait was of Mortimer!' I protested. 'Old Lord Hammerford could hardly know that Mortimer's replacement would also be called Mortimer, now could he, in all conscience? True, he might find a portrait somewhere of a man with the same name as the new doorman, but that too would be a coincidence. And the new man might have an odd name, one so odd that no portait of anyone with such a name exists in any public art gallery.'

'True, but then this is merely one link in the chain, and the final link at that,' Holmes told me. 'Were anything to happen to Mortimer, the previous Lord Hammerford need only amend the last couple of clues. He need not use the same portrait trick, need he? He could, as a last resort, merely have given the new man's name directly in the last clue, or else used a very simple code, as before. No, there is no real difficulty about that, provided always that coincidence did not enter too greatly into the matter.' He glanced out of the window, and added, 'Ah! We are catching up with Sir George. He had only a short start, and his cab is neither so well driven nor provided with as good horseflesh as your carriage, Sir James.'

He was right in this. In the crowded streets we were necessarily obliged to remain in second place, but when once we found a relatively unfrequented stretch of road Sir James's driver was able to pull out and we soon sailed past Sir George's cab. Sir George himself looked out at us as we passed him, and called furiously to his driver. It was, I think, a good thing that we could not hear exactly what he said, but the sense was fairly obvious.

The positions were now reversed, and once we were back into the stream of traffic Sir George's cab could not hope to do more than keep up with us, and even that became increasingly difficult. 'We are well ahead,' said Holmes after another glance through the window, 'but we must be ready to jump out when we are somewhere near, for I suspect that Sir George will not hesitate to cover the last few yards on foot if needs be.'

We turned into St James's, and the streets were less crowded. Holmes glanced backwards again, and grunted in annoyance. 'He is gaining on us,' he said.

We drew up all of a sudden before the door of the club, and Holmes was out of the carriage before we had fully stopped. Sir James followed more sedately, while I waited on the kerb to see what Sir George intended. Like Holmes, he was out of his cab before it had stopped, and he fairly raced across the pavement, heedless of the cabbie's request for payment, and only slowing down when he reached me. 'Ah, Doctor Watson,' said he, civilly enough, but with ill-suppressed annoyance in his tone. 'This means, I take it, that I have failed?'

'By a very short head, Sir George.'

He laughed. 'Well, at the very least you will hardly begrudge me a look at what I have missed?'

I hesitated, then, thinking it unworthy to suspect him of villainy at this last stage of the search, I nodded and stood aside to let him enter before me. Holmes and Sir James were standing in front of Mortimer's counter when Sir George and I strolled into the lobby. Holmes glanced round. 'Ah, Sir George,' said he, 'just pipped at the post, you see! Mortimer is just now reclaiming the Hammerford inheritance from what he is pleased to label his cubbyhole. You, I take it, wish to see what it is you have lost?'

'If it's no trouble to you.' The words were said lightly enough, but there was no mistaking the bitter disappointment in Sir George's voice.

Mortimer emerged from his inner sanctum, a large parcel

in his hands. It was evidently weighty, for the poor old fellow could scarcely lift it. Holmes moved forward, and took the package from him. 'Well, gentlemen —' he began, but that was all he got out before Sir George had snatched the parcel from his arms, and pushed Holmes aside.

Holmes cannoned into Sir James, who in turn knocked me flying. I saw Sir George take to his heels, and remember thinking that he was a decent sprinter, handicapped as he was by the heavy package. I quickly recovered my wits sufficiently to go to assist Holmes and Sir James to their feet.

Holmes, however, shook off my proffered arm. 'Get after him, Watson!' he cried. 'We're unhurt, and the treasure is the thing now!'

All three of us raced out of the door, but then came to an abrupt halt at the sight of Sir George, lying in the gutter and rubbing his head. Holmes bent down and helped him to his feet. 'One last try, Sir George? But what happened?'

'We've all been done, I fear!' said Sir George ruefully, but with a valiant attempt at a smile. He waved a hand down the road, and we looked where he pointed, to see what had been Sir George's cab rattling along at a smart pace.

'Quick!' said Holmes, leaping into Sir James's carriage. Sir George did not hesitate, but sprang up onto the driver's seat, pushing Sir James's startled coachman to one side, and whipping up the horses. Sir James and I had our work cut out to scramble into the carriage as it set off in pursuit of the cab with its priceless cargo.

Whatever his other faults, Sir George was a splendid driver, but even so I do not think we would have caught up with the other cab were it not for that old enemy, traffic. I looked out of the window, to see some sort of altercation taking place on top of the cab which we were following. I take it the driver had remonstrated with the villains, and they had climbed out on to the roof of his cab, and were attempting to force him to go faster, or take some risk that was unpalatable to him, or something of that sort. Anyway, the poor driver was literally flung off the cab into the gutter, but to judge by his language as we sailed past, he was not too badly hurt.

Thanks to Sir George, we were now gaining on them slightly, and when a large delivery van emerged from a side road right in front of the cab, causing it to slow down suddenly, Sir George was able to bring our carriage along-side and force the cab off the road, on to the pavement, and into a shop-front.

As the startled shopkeeper emerged, Holmes and Sir George rushed to the cab and tackled the villains. I saw one of the gang leap from the cab and hare off down the street. 'After him, Watson!' cried Holmes, and I took to my heels in hot pursuit.

After a dozen yards, the man I was following turned, and slowed down, as if expecting something to happen behind us. I instinctively did as he had done, looked back, and saw another of the villains standing on the roof of the cab, the famous parcel clutched in a brawny arm. He called some-thing unintelligible to my man, and made as if to throw the parcel.

The memory of a painful incident involving a large and uncivil Irish forward at Twickenham came irresistibly to my mind. I turned to face my man, lowered my head, and charged. He was evidently not expecting this, and went flying with a great gasp indicative of surprise, pain and anger. I turned round again, and caught the package fair and square as it flew through the air towards me.

A languid gentleman on the pavement nearby, who had watched these proceedings with not the least hint of emotion, nodded at me and said, 'Well caught, sir! But damned if you shouldn't be sent off for that low punch.'

'This is a criminal investigation, sir,' I told him angrily. 'I'll thank you to keep your impertinent remarks to yourself!'

ELEVEN

'**A** very satisfactory conclusion, Holmes,' I said, filling glasses for him, Sir James and myself.

'It is certainly a happy ending,' said Holmes, a touch of cynicism in his voice. 'That should please you, Doctor, and your readers.'

'And what of that?' I asked him. 'By the law of averages, there should be as many happy as unhappy endings.'

Holmes shook his head. 'Without wishing to offend our guest,' said he, with a nod towards Sir James, 'I am still unconvinced by this business of establishing one's legitimacy by a test of skill.'

'Oh, I thought we had dealt with all that nonsense,' said Sir James. 'It is surely as an intellectual challenge that you should judge our little adventure.'

'In that light, of course, it was not entirely unsuccessful, or devoid of interest,' said Holmes.

Sir James went on, 'As for young Lord Hammerford, I have hopes that he will grow to manhood and eventual old age quite unaware of his grandfather's suspicions. Totally unfounded suspicions, I may add.'

Holmes sat forward in his chair. 'Oh? You are certain of that?' he asked.

Sir James nodded. 'The august gentleman concerned has

told me that there was no hint of impropriety, and that is good enough for me. As it should be for you.'

'Well, it is,' said Holmes. He sighed. 'If ever we can dispense with these ranks and titles, how much happier we should be! Was it not Pepys who remarked that there are so many titles that plain unaffected "Mr" is itself something of a distinction?'

'Henry Fearon, surely,' said Sir James with a frown. 'I know that Pepys made a great fuss when he was first called "Esquire", though I would not argue as to the precise attribution.'

'Surgeons, of course, insist upon "Mr",' I added. 'And for a rather curious and interesting reason.'

'Which is known to every schoolboy,' said Holmes. 'Indeed, I sometimes wonder if the story is not part of the treatment, a species of faith healing.'

'Don't dismiss faith healing too lightly, Holmes,' I told him. 'I remember one old *fakir* in Firozabad —' I broke off as I saw the others glowering at me. 'But that's neither here nor there,' I added hastily. 'Tell me, Sir James, what is to become of the lad? Young Lord Hammerford, I mean.'

'Now, that is a fairy-tale ending,' said Sir James with a laugh, 'for Sir George and Lady Lewis have taken him under their wing.'

'You trust them to look after him?' I asked.

'Implicitly. Oh, I've had my differences with Sir George, of course, but you only have to see the look in his eye when he's with the lad. And Lady Lewis is delighted with the little chap.'

'And the money?' asked Holmes prosaically.

'I did what you suggested, and negotiated with Sir George

at the last,' said Sir James. 'After all, if the lad were farmed out with strangers, they'd expect payment, and there would be no guarantee that they'd look after him properly, much less that they'd show him any real love or affection. Sir George was reasonable enough in his demands, and I flatter myself I've not done too badly for Lord Hammerford.'

In the event, he was right, though of course we could not know it then. Lord Hammerford is now a man of three-and-twenty, and last week I had the honour of attending the christening of his first child, a son. Sir James was there, of course, and Sir George, the latter with a proud look in his eye. 'I'm devilish pleased it's a boy,' he whispered to me as we stood together in the little church.

'Carry on the name, as it were?' I asked, for the lad was to be called George as well as James.

'That, too, of course,' said Sir George, embarrassed.

I stared at him.

'Fact is, I had a small wager on the outcome with one of the chaps at the club. You won't say anything, of course?'

'You may rely upon me,' I told him.